D. M...   ...rs in the
Dioce...   ...servant.
Her f...   ...nd as a
mature student she took a second degree in Theology
... London University She has also taught at a
... including St Paul's Girls' in
Lo... overlooking the Thames in
Greenwich, with her lurcher bitch.

Also by D. M. Greenwood

Clerical Errors
Unholy Ghosts
Idol Bones
Holy Terrors
Every Deadly Sin

Mortal Spoils

D. M. Greenwood

HEADLINE

First published in 1996
by HEADLINE BOOK PUBLISHING

First published in paperback in 1996
by HEADLINE BOOK PUBLISHING

10 9 8 7 6 5 4 3 2 1

ISBN 0 7472 5190 8

Printed and bound in Great Britain by
Cox & Wyman Ltd, Reading, Berks

HEADLINE BOOK PUBLISHING
A division of Hodder Headline PLC
338 Euston Road
London NW1 3BH

For David Herbert

Contents

CHAPTER ONE

The Body

'What does "Venerable" mean?'

'Downpipes and gutters. Archdeacon. Sort of works manager. Supposed to be able to read the bottom line. Every diocese has one or two. They come next to bishops.'

'What do I call them?'

'Mr or Archdeacon or sir.' Sergeant Ashwood, ex-Royal Artillery, currently head porter of Ecclesia Place, Westminster, looked down on his raw recruit, under-doorman Trace, with some misgiving. The lad was fresh from five unsuccessful years at South-West London Comprehensive where, clearly, they had taught him nothing about the structure of English society. He had a ring in his left ear and his fair hair was long on top and short like fur and darker round the back and sides. His black porter's jacket had been tailored for a bigger man. It hung on him like washing on a line.

Trace pushed his finger down the list. 'Right Reverend,' he spelt out with incredulity.

'Bishop. Ours have purple shirts and cassocks. The Roman Catholics don't. They have black. It's confusing when you have these ecumenical dos.'

'Ecu what?' Trace wondered if he really wanted this job.

'More than one branch of the Church. Like Methodists, and Greek Orthodox and that.'

Trace didn't know about them either. 'What do they do, then, bishops?'

'Bishops run dioceses. Groups of churches,' Ashwood hurried on to forestall the impending question, 'all in the same part of the country. Like counties.' Had the lad heard of counties?

Trace had heard of counties, it seemed. 'Very Reverend?'

'Ah, that's deans. They run cathedrals. Chief church in any diocese where the bishop has his seat. Smoothies. Sometimes scholars but most often only pretending.' Ashwood's brother was a verger at Medwich. He had inside information. 'The evangelical ones will ask you your Christian name and call you by it. Don't try the same back. You call them Dean or Mr Dean. What *is* your Christian name, Trace?'

'Eh?'

'Your first name.'

Trace knew this one. 'Kevin,' said Kevin proudly. 'After Kevin O'Con.'

'Yes. Pity it isn't more Christian.'

Trace was hurt. 'Well, what's yours then?'

'Daniel. As in the lions' den.' Years of church parades had left their mark on Ashwood.

'Where?'

'Forget it. What's next?' Ashwood peered at the list.

'Canon. *Canon*?'

'Two sorts. Hardworking parish priests. Sort of MC for service in the field. Called honorary. And the other sort, called residentiary, help deans run cathedrals. Bone idle. Big beautiful houses in cathedral closes, large cars and light liturgical duties.'

'Can anyone apply?'

'No one applies for jobs in the Church of England. You catch a bishop's eye.'

'Most Reverend.' Kevin was tired after so much concentration.

'Archbishop. The top brass. Field marshals. Only two of them. Canterbury and York. York's coming for today's big do. Addressed as "your grace".'

'Jesus,' said Kevin.

'I wouldn't use too much language, laddie, the clergy don't like it.'

'They use enough of it themselves.' Kevin felt he was being bright and keeping his end up in this strange world.

'Keep your mouth shut and your eyes open. It's bound to be a bit foreign to you first time round. You just learn the faces of the regulars so you can greet 'em by name. They like that.'

'They don't half think well of themselves.'

'Why shouldn't they?' Ashwood felt his own authority was bound up with his employers. He was part of the system. He had his place. 'And do your jacket up. It looks horrible like that.'

'It's hot and it doesn't fit,' Kevin objected.

'I said, do it up,' Ashwood snapped. 'You're the front line. People what don't know no better could judge the whole of the Church of England by you being the first thing they meet across the desk here. Appearances matter.'

Kevin did up his buttons as though they were unfamiliar bits of technology. Just as well the lad should know how things stood, Ashwood felt.

'Any tips?' Kevin inquired, searching for a ray of sunshine.

'You should be so lucky. Not so much as a florin has come my way in going on six years.'

'Flinty?'

'Some are. Some of 'em haven't got much themselves. I've never seen such a set of down-at-heel scruffy shoes as you get in here.' Sergeant Ashwood had military standards in leather goods. His own boots shone, as they had throughout his service. 'I reckon they think 'cos it's the Church you work for, you do it for charity like. They don't take no account of wives and families.'

'You got a wife and family, Dan?'

4

'I got grandchildren I like to spend on now and again.'

'I ain't got no wife and family. But I could do with a bit in advance.'

'You 'aven't done nothing yet. You get paid Friday same as everybody else. Now just you learn that list and keep your mind on your job. There'll be a lot of strangers coming and going for this here meeting. Everyone what comes in, signs in, and everyone what goes out, signs out. Right?'

'Right.'

'The telly'll be here round fiveish so they can film the end of the meeting round seven.' Ashwood consulted his clipboard. He felt safe with orders for the day in his hand. Even so it was going to be a strain, he could tell. Canon Clutch was a nasty-tempered beggar if anything went wrong and often if everything went right too. 'You'll be able to tell them, the telly lot. They look a lot different from the clergy. More casual and richer. Cost a mint, some of that gear. And they bring a lot of stuff with them. Cameras and sound stuff and such.'

'Telly, eh?'

'*News at Ten.*'

Sergeant Ashwood was impressed. Kevin was impressed.

'They'll want to film the Archimandrite,' Ashwood said.

'What's an Archi . . .?'

'Foreign. Same as our Archbishop.'

'What's he here for then?'

'They're going to sign something. A treaty or whatever. Him and the Archbishop.'

'So it's, like, quite important, this place?' Kevin was readjusting his perspective on his first job which he'd advertised to his friends in Betterhouse, the other side of the Thames, merely as 'across the water', not daring to add it was to do with the Church.

'Important?' Ashwood was outraged. Thirty-two years in Her Majesty's armed forces, senior NCO with an (almost) unblemished record of conduct. Did the boy think he, Ashwood, would take a job other than in the first rank of things? He'd been offered the Institute of Directors. But Ashwood knew more about British society than that. The Church of England had the Queen as its head. There was history and ritual going for the Church. 'This place,' he said, fixing his eyes on the 1930s bleached oak panelling of the entrance hall of Ecclesia Place, 'this here is centuries old. This is where the power is. What the Houses of Parliament are to ordinary life, Ecclesia Place is to the life of the Church of England. It's the centre of the worldwide communion of the Anglican Church,' he quoted. 'The heart of the empire,' he improvised. 'The commonwealth,' he amended. 'So nothing at all's got to go wrong today when we're entertaining foreigners,' he concluded.

Three storeys above Ashwood and Kevin's reception desk, Tom Logg swung his revolving chair from his desktop computer to his laptop computer and felt peaceful and fulfilled as the patience cards came up on the screen. Like Kevin, Ecclesia Place was Tom's first real job. Unlike Kevin, he had no doubt about his ability to fill his role. His subjects at university had been Business Studies and French. Ecclesia Place had all the features enumerated in his first-year textbook *What Is An Institution*? It manufactured its own business. It took in bits of the outside world and processed them into Ecclesia Place-shaped tablets and then swallowed them. The means of tablet-making were memoranda or, on more demanding topics, briefing papers. From attic to cellar, via an unreliable internal communications network of telephones and in trays, it kept itself in work. Part civil service, part club, part college, it had its ethos. Its regular members, known as 'established', greeted by name by Ashwood, possessed a patina, Tom had detected. The Place, as the established called it, had its pride, its traditional ways of doing things and its own jargon to baffle and deflate outsiders. Above all, it had a distinguished architectural presence. The structure and values of clerical culture were all proclaimed in the architecture. That is to say, it was impressive, it was expensive, and it didn't work.

To others of a more metaphysical turn of mind the building was an analogue of the inner, the religious life. It had been designed from foundations to door handles in the 1930s by a single architect. Entrances, staircases, corridors, windows and lifts formed a landscape of event and feeling far beyond bricks and mortar: here we meet, there we part, here we eat, there we debate. It was a cosmos, an orderly world – but easy, like the religious life, to get lost in.

To strangers, certainly, the building was discouraging. Miles of expensively panelled corridors with identical rooms opening off them and staircases secreted behind doors which looked as though they must lead to rooms, deceived those not in the know. Direction boards so unobtrusive as to evade the harassed eye, or bearing a single enigmatic arrow, ensured that anyone without an established guide got lost. The traveller then had to humble himself to knock on a door and ask for directions. Often he would be met with a fish-eyed occupant disturbed in the middle of solving the secret of the universe.

The corridors were without windows. The external world was excluded as though it was feared that perceptions might be contaminated by reality. Gallery led on from gallery, dome from dome. The landmarks, a mosaic walled conference hall in the Byzantine taste and a tiny chapel in Victorian Gothic, were met with relief by wanderers but they were no guarantee of ultimate salvation. For, once these were left behind, visitors would be plunged once more into the long soundless corridors imaging one version of eternity.

Tom looked round his office. It had been his first challenge in his new job. There had been nothing in it when he'd first come into post except a table. He'd set himself twenty-four hours to get it properly equipped for work. Knowing nothing about the institution (there had been no induction course), with no contacts or network to rely on, no favours to call in, he'd managed to get a filing cabinet, a desk, a revolving chair, a phone and his two computers. In the course of his efforts he'd memorised the topography of the building from top floor to crypt library, sorted out the institution's financial procedures and made a friend of his boss's secretary. He'd made a good professional start, he reckoned.

Now he consulted his computer's digital clock. It flashed the date at him, Monday 4th October, Feast of St Francis of Assisi, as well as the time. He was hungry. He could do with elevenses but it was only ten past ten. Tom was almost permanently hungry. He ate four times a day if he could possibly manage it. He had huge feet and very long wrists and a neck which sprang like a sapling out of his collar. There was no ounce of spare flesh on his bony frame. An oblong head with black hair cut *en brosse* like a hogged mane gave him a slightly foreign appearance. His lips were pursed as though to deal with the demands of the French language at which he was competent. One attraction of the job at Ecclesia Place was that there was a canteen on site which was permanently in session from 8 a.m. to 8 p.m. Tom liked that.

As his fingers flew over the keyboard in his tiny room on the top floor, he liked to think of the refectory a lift ride down on the ground floor, humming away with tea urns and grills. He felt himself supported and scaffolded by a great warm cloud of food-laden air. He was often the first customer for breakfast and the last out from supper twelve hours later. In between he hoped for, but did not always manage to achieve, lunch and tea. At night in his brother's cold basement flat at the other end of Victoria, he slept intensely, as though dead, for about five hours between midnight and dawn. The rest of the time he worked. He had no lawn to mow, no wife to please, no children to ferry, no parish to nurse. One project after another dropped into his in tray to be translated into memoranda, briefing papers, background papers, scenarios, alternative scenarios, business plans, appraisals of business plans.

His father, finding the fatigue of returning to the same woman every night more than he could bear, had left home early in his marriage. The task of seeing his mother right had fallen upon Tom. He had worked like a Trojan at school, at the supermarket on Saturdays and, later, at his provincial university. By the time he'd reached manhood, he'd got into the habit of working. He was perpetually surprised how little other people, especially other people at the Place, especially other people in the top echelons of the Place, actually did. They left letters unanswered, attended meetings without a briefing note to bless themselves with, seemed to think it was a form of cheating to acquire relevant knowledge when new demands were made on them, and eschewed training of any kind as though it might lead to death.

Tom was not censorious. He made inventories not judgements. Clerical culture was just one more heading in the textbook he would eventually write for trainee managers. He'd chosen Ecclesia Place partly because it had an ethos which did not figure in his Business Studies course. He knew a lot about management structures at Ford and Nissan and workplace values at Lloyd's and the Norwich Union, but the Church of England was uncharted waters. Here be dragons, he told himself as he set out on his chosen career. He was already on his third course of communication skills. He'd studied best practice in team building (he didn't have a team as yet), chairmanship (he'd chaired at least one meeting so far), time management (very useful couple of courses those), and he reckoned he could meet all-comers in planning, policy-making and monitoring.

He had been in post just long enough (ten weeks) to begin to wonder whether the organisation was really making the best use of him, whether in fact it deserved him. But he wouldn't be hasty. He was embarked on a learning curve. He hadn't got the organisation mapped as yet. He was thorough. Before he'd finished, he'd know everyone, their job descriptions, their performance indicators, their strengths and weaknesses. His research tasks, prioritised and computerised on his private disk accessed only by the password 'cleric', were, firstly, to find out what the aims and objectives of the institution were; secondly, whether it had any strategies for realising these; and thirdly, whether it had any forward financial planning to cost the hypothetical strategies. To be honest, he hadn't actually got too far with any of this as yet. He simply must push on because he had to write it up for *Modern Management*'s Christmas number in a couple of months' time. He hoped perhaps today's visit, upon which so much, he was given to suppose, depended for the Church of England, might reveal at least something which could count as an aim. He made notes and kept careful case studies. Today's operation was codenamed 'Archiman'.

Tom reported to the Chief Secretary to the Diet, the CSD, Canon Clutch. He'd got the latter's work habits taped but not what the work actually was. Canon Clutch came in at ten-thirty, looked through the mail which Tom had sorted for him, indicated the nature of his answers on tape which Tom then worked up into letters, did *The Times* crossword and departed for lunch at twelve. Sometimes he wrote a letter to *The Times* and in this way contributed, Tom gathered, to both politics and scholarship in the Anglican mode. At four he might or might not reappear to sign a letter and at four-thirty he was on his way to Paddington for the five three to Thame.

Much the same pattern was followed by the rest of the hierarchy. The trick, Tom had noted with approval, (its simplicity and symmetry appealed to him) was to clock in ten minutes before your superior came in and to leave ten minutes after he (there were no women above the level of typist) had gone. Tom was the sole exception to this ritual. He was in at 8 a.m. and left twelve hours later.

He seized his pocket electronic organiser and clicked the display to check his day's work. It read: 'AM: check porters, Can Clutch, Arch brief, conf rm. PM Archie, TV press Archi, food for all.' It was going to be a full day, he observed with pleasure. Lots and lots to do. He reached for his mobile phone and made for the door. Much could be accomplished while walking the corridors of ecclesiastical power.

Canon Clutch, midway between Tom and the porters, that is to say on the desirable first floor of Ecclesia Place, in his room overlooking the Thames, admitted with reluctance that he could not complete the crossword from the clue 'Holy Book not quite long enough for eighth of May'. He pushed the paper from him and looked with distaste at the large desk diary with gold-edged leaves and morocco cover and sighed. It was going to be a busy day. He could see no way out of it. Even if it meant a lot of time spent with the great and the good (and the great and the good were Canon Clutch's speciality, his *raison d'être*), still there would be longueurs when he would have to be about but not actually the centre of affairs. The trouble with arch bishops was they took precedence; they expected every- one else to defer to them. Even someone as genuinely humble as Papworth of York would naturally rise to the top of everyone else's agenda. Canon Clutch had worked with him over the years and found his tall, spare figure in the classical Anglican mould something of an affront to his own style. Canon Clutch himself,

was tall enough to be a bishop, but his large head with
its wealth of silvery hair worn rather long and his
florid complexion looked more worldly than ecclesiastical. His dress was immaculate. It resembled a successful lawyer's, that of a high court judge, he told himself,
rather than a cleric. Indeed, when he had first come
into post fifteen years ago, he'd discovered where the
most eminent lawyers went for their tailoring and
followed suit. This end of Victoria abutting on to Westminster was awash with lawyers. He felt, without
precisely defining it to himself, that they had real power
while he had only a second-rate kind. He did not dwell
on this uncomfortable perception though sometimes it
crept up on him like unforeseen indigestion.

Kenneth Clutch was in some respects the human
counterpart of the building. He was his own architect
and he'd attended to every detail. He had learned early
in life to convert fear into anger and communicate his
anger in such a way that others were frightened of
him. Just so had he imposed his created self upon the
world. He was, no one could deny, immensely impressive. He could not be said to be a liar since he sincerely
believed what he felt and therefore what he said. In his
presence few doubted the truth of his view. He had
early in his career espied and fixed his world, the world
of official culture where gentlemen were recognisable
by their dress and speech and deferred to by others of
different dress and speech. This world had disappeared
in the course of Clutch's career. His was, surely, the
last generation (he was sixty-two) which aspired to

gentility by copying its accoutrements. In the Church of England, or anyway in its upper echelons, he was not alone, but he was, he prided himself, among the most successful. He had never run a parish, never organised so much as a church fete, had taken a theology degree forty years ago and neither read a book nor embarked on any course of training subsequently, but he was where he was, at the highest pinnacle of the management of the Church, by impressing the right people and doing the done thing. Perhaps only an institution which had interpreted its role as being one of ruling, because it was so closely connected with rulers, could have bred and nurtured Canon Clutch. Perhaps he was its reward.

Within the safe doors of the Church, along the quiet, busy corridors of Ecclesia Place, it was possible, it was easy, to imagine that the traditional culture prevailed, was important, was the only importance. Of course, there was a price to pay. If you live in a bubble of illusion you must not step outside the bubble, and all that enters it must be processed and refined to fit the illusion. Canon Clutch had a number of strategies to see that all was kept as it traditionally had been. He commanded the language and categories for dismissing the too importunate, too ragged external world. 'Tenth-rate, no clout, not the brightest of boys' were terms with which he kept the bridge. Lately, snuffing a wind of change in the culture, he had begun to espouse the modern jargon, the bullish, clubby cliché drawn from the world of the military, finance and the media.

He picked it up in his club, Brooks (not the
Athenaeum, which he'd early recognised was for the
dim, the tenth-rate). The Falklands war had given him
the term 'task force', financiers taught him to talk
about downsizing and back burners. Clergy with less
time than himself to study the latest verbal fashion
were impressed and somehow comforted. There was at
least one of them, and one at the top too, who knew the
modern world and could cope with it. Thus, cleverly,
had Canon Clutch learnt to have his cake and eat it; he
despised the modern world and it terrified him, but he
knew its language and many of its leading figures. And
that was what counted.

He looked out on the khaki water of the river. The
Place possessed a paved courtyard abutting the river
and open to the public. The large, tough leaves of the
plane trees swirled into the gutters and heavy autumn
rain beat on the windows of his office. Outside he could
just distinguish the figures of the two resident tramps
huddled on the bench overlooking the embankment.
God knew what they were doing there in this weather.

Clutch wore a half-hunter. He took it out and consulted it. The Archbishop would be here at about three
forty, the Archimandrite at four. Difficult for meals
and hospitality, that timing. In the end he'd decided to
serve afternoon tea at four. That blazing idiot Logg had
been told to lay on the cucumber sandwiches and
China and Indian. Show the little foreign man what
the best people did in this seat of power. That would
leave about two hours for talking and the official

signing of the concordat at about seven. He planned to get the Archimandrite back to Brown's as soon as maybe and then invite Papworth to dine with him at the club. He'd need to fill him in on one or two matters before posting him back on the train for York around tenish. Logg was dealing with the press release and he'd promised Archie Douglas he'd wheel on the Archimandrite and the Archbishop for the TV interview before they left. Meanwhile, however, there was the Place General Purposes Committee to deal with and its little domestic agenda. Indeed, if he mistook him not, there was the murmur of manly voices in the outer office already.

'Come in, David, Tim, and Christopher too,' he said heartily, beaming on the trio of dog collars converging on his door. 'Has anyone got eight across?'

Tom Logg, snatching a late, substantial lunch in the almost empty refectory, checked his organiser. Everything had been accomplished by two-fifteen. Pretty good, he congratulated himself, mopping up the remains of loin of pork with a supplementary bread roll. The posse of French nuns had dabbed their dainty lips, risen as one woman and glided noiselessly out. The American evangelists, dressed in dog collars and camping gear, had made an uproariously cheerful exit, calling out names, addresses and telephone numbers as they went. The four members of Canon Truegrave's staff (Eastern European Affairs) who looked and acted like spies, heads close together, unEnglish clothes, had disappeared suddenly like pigeons, each flying its own way.

At this hour the place was practically deserted. The staff had melted back into their own squalid quarters behind the kitchen. The lady on the tea urn came out every now and again to draw stewed refreshment from the communal pot for her colleagues. The new lad from the porters' desk had finished off a plate of beans and chips almost the size of Tom's own and scooted out when Sergeant Ashwood had put his head round the door and looked at him. Over the far side was the figure, so unobtrusive as to be almost invisible, of the librarian and archivist, Canon Teape. Tom liked Teape. He was the only person who had spoken to him outside the call of duty during his first week in post. They had shared a table and a late lunch hour on his first Friday.

'I'm Teape,' Teape had said cautiously, eyeing Tom from behind his copy of the *Antiquarian Bookseller*, once he had made sure the other was indeed staying at the table.

'Logg,' said Tom. 'Tom Logg. Canon Clutch's assistant,' he added, having learnt that clergy can't identify laymen except in relation to their clerical masters. 'I'm new.'

'Which way do you start off with people?' Teape had asked.

'Sorry?' Tom had paused in mid-swipe of steak and kidney pudding.

'I mean, do you start by assuming that they're all

18

highly intelligent and totally honest and then let them prove you wrong? Or do you go the other way? Take it they're idle and stupid until they give you evidence to the contrary?'

This degree of self-analysis was not too familiar to Tom but he had cast it immediately into business studies terms and realised that as far as human relations skills were concerned, it was quite a useful analytical tool and worthy of his consideration.

'I think I proceed on the first assumption,' he answered truthfully.

'You'll have a lot to learn here,' said Teape and retired behind his journal.

Since that time a couple of months ago he had addressed no further word to Tom. Now he rose and left the refectory still clutching, Tom noticed, his periodical.

Tom leaned back in his chair and stretched his very long arms above his head and back behind him. He considered what he could do next. It would be defeat indeed if he could not fill the next hour before the arrival of the Archbishop. Check the conference room. Drinking water and carafe. Of course. He sprang up happily and loped off down the room, up the back staircase and along the corridor. It was an inside corridor with no outside windows. The lights, set at parsimonious intervals of about twenty yards, produced a dim religious glow. One of the bulbs needed replacing. Tom tapped the requirements into his organiser. The corridor was quite deserted. There was an after-lunch stupor oozing from under the closed doors of offices and seminar rooms. Tom turned sharp right and the corridor opened out into a stairhead and gallery, round the wall of which were hung portraits of past archbishops. It was one of Tom's favourite areas. Portraits ranged in style from the late seventeenth century, icons of the Erastian religious life, via the Victorian romantic to the modern functional imitations of photographs. A particularly good example of the Victorian crop was Archbishop Tuddenham, an obscure Archbishop of York in the early nineteenth century, depicted on a Regency Gothick throne with mitres for finials. It reminded Tom of a portrait he'd once seen of Edmund Kean playing Lear. Something in the wildness of the silver hair escaping from underneath the mitre, the concave face and dark, harrowed eyes, the clawlike hands grasping the arms of the throne imparted an immensely theatrical air to the whole composition.

Tom stopped at the end of the corridor to admire this dramatic masterpiece. He let his eye wander over it and then come to rest on the chair beneath it. The chair was not empty. It was occupied by a thickset figure in a dark suit, his head sunk forward on to his chest. From beneath the heavy black beard spreading round the lower part of the face could be seen the silver pectoral cross of a bishop. One thick finger bore what could have been an episcopal ring.

Tom approached the figure carefully, mindful of the old adage about letting sleeping bishops lie. When he was within a couple of feet of the chair, he cleared his throat. There was no response. Tom was nonplussed. He'd not read anything in his business studies course which gave him a formula for dealing with clerics asleep in security cleared zones. The Archbishop and the Archimandrite had both required the security to be stringent. Who was allowed where and when was all charted on the plan in Tom's office and it didn't include an unknown bishop slumbering in a chair outside the conference room a couple of hours before countdown.

He stepped a little nearer. Something in the angle of the man's head struck him. Very gently he put his hand on the shoulder and shook it. The figure, as though dislodged from a niche, slid calamitously forward onto the floor.

It did not need any business studies manual to tell Tom that this priest was dead

CHAPTER TWO

The Stowage

Theodora Braithwaite, a woman of about thirty in deacon's orders in the Church of England, looked out of the window of her flat in Betterhouse on the south bank of the Thames on Monday evening. It was quite dark at ten o'clock. The only light came from the glow, which never leaves the London sky, reflected off the river. Two adolescent foxes were making their way down the alley, cuffing each other in comradely fashion. As they reached the end of the cul-de-sac, a dog barked. With no change of pace or hesitation, one fox squeezed under the fence and the other posted himself through the gaping hole of the vandalised letterbox of the defunct warehouse opposite. The alley which had seemed populated, now felt empty. A smell of wet plane leaves drifted in on the mild autumn air. It was very quiet. The warehouses on either side of the terrace in which the flat was situated screened out the roar of London's traffic. Such peace, such pleasure, she thought. How can I be grateful enough for this sanctuary?

She withdrew her head from the open window and surveyed her domain. There was no furniture, only packing cases of books dotted over the floor of the room which ran from front to back of the first floor of the house. At either end was an uncurtained window. Halfway down, a door stood open onto a lobby, in which could be glimpsed a stone sink and a ferocious Baby Belling. All was in a state of decay. Lincrusta wallpaper flapped loose from bulging plaster. A dangerous swathe of woven purple flex was pinned in loops towards a single electric fitment in the centre of the ceiling. The floor was bare boards of a greyish splintery kind.

'Lovely,' said Theodora aloud. She meant, just enough for her needs.

It was her first night in her own place. This was the first time in her entire life that she had not had to consider the needs of anyone but herself. Is this to be really grown up, she wondered. Ever since she had left her father's rectory, first for boarding school then for university, she'd shared accommodation. Theological college, a clergy house in Nairobi and latterly the basement of the vicarage of St Sylvester's Church in Betterhouse had found her carefully, courteously putting others' convenience before her own. Now she was free. Her vicar, Geoffrey Brighouse, had recently taken it into his head to marry and his wife was not for keeping curates in the basement, especially when the curate was a woman. Theodora had had to look for alternative lodgings.

She'd been touched to find how many of the parishioners of this diverse parish had been eager to have her. She'd been offered rooms in the high street with the Robinsons who made frequent trips to the Caribbean and mistakenly thought she liked young children, of which they had many. Then there'd been a flat over the Chinese chippy's, tentatively suggested because, though they wouldn't normally have considered taking anyone outside their family, they were looking for someone quiet and they reckoned they didn't come quieter than Theodora. Even the Archdeacon had intimated that since the diocese had a duty to house her, he would be happy to help so had she thought of moving into the spare room in the Foundation of St Sylvester? It was, after all, next door to the church and hence convenient for her duties. The Foundation, to the work of which Theodora contributed a day a week in addition to her parish tasks, was a retreat house and centre for Christian therapy. This meant, in effect, that it sheltered a shifting population of people whose needs were unassuageable. The director of the centre, the Reverend Doctor Gilbert Racy, had clearly been in two minds about the Archdeacon's suggestion. On the one hand it would be quite nice to have an unpaid, dependable night nurse continually on tap. On the other, his was a bachelor and, indeed, celibate establishment which he hated to have disturbed. On the whole, regretfully, he declined to have Theodora. She turned with relief to walking the parish to see where she would really like to live. She took her time. She knew by now that a house is a way of life, it carries moral as well as aesthetic values.

Betterhouse in Pepys' time had been a ferry across the Thames for travellers from the Channel ports making for Westminster. In the nineteenth century the railway had arrived and increased both the population and the river traffic. The Church of St Sylvester had been built to serve the neighbourhood. Wharves and warehouses followed, blocking off most of the river which remained accessible only by way of an occasional set of steps. When the river trade declined in the sixties of the twentieth century, these remained and rotted. The Victorian terraces, which had come with the railway, had filled with every race and culture. The tower blocks, the most recent addition to the landscape, guarded the outskirts of the borough as, in former times, wall and ramparts might have done.

It was, of course, towards the river that Theodora in the end gravitated. She'd stumbled upon the Stowage eighteen months ago when she'd first come into the parish. It was guarded by a one-way system and its status as a cul-de-sac. It had been evening in spring when she had turned the corner, smelt the river, and heard the pluck and suck of the tide on the steps at the end of the alley. But the terrace of dilapidated houses was uninhabited. No people meant no pastoral duties.

She'd stayed for a moment to take in the cats and rats and decaying tyres which littered the weedy cobbles, before turning back to more frequented ways.

Now, needing lodgings, she had returned. She knew at once that this was her habitat. The end house must have been the ferryman's. It was lower than the terrace and timber-framed with a tile roof. It was also decayed beyond redemption. The adjoining buildings, however, looked more hopeful. They were later, eighteenth-century, slate-roofed artisans' dwellings, each distinguished by a different design of fanlight over the front door. A shallow brick pediment unified them into a row. She squeezed through the door of the end one and surveyed the interior. The cellars were supported on the masts of sailing ships. The windows were broken. The roof had buddleia growing from the guttering. Ferns decorated the soil pipe. The drains were not what the health and safety man would have wished. The following morning she spent twenty minutes with Gilbert Racy, a reliable fount of local and ecclesiastical gossip, and discovered that the owners were the St Sylvester's Trust. Their affairs were dealt with by Ecclesia Place. She did some telephoning and finally sought out the Archdeacon. They concluded a deal. Theodora knew she was being cheated: rent plus a full repairing lease would bankrupt her. He was an old hand.

'We *could* stretch to a new roof,' the Archdeacon admitted.

'And a phone,' Theodora bargained despairingly.

The Archdeacon did a calculation. 'You're on.'

It was the best she could hope for. She knew the Archdeacon relied on her putting the place in order and then moving on to a new living. She hoped, God willing, that she might disappoint him.

So here she was, two months and a new roof later. Monday was her day off. She'd spent a lot of time and money on paint and Teepol. Furniture, no stick of which she possessed, would not be her first concern. There was no hurry. The religious life was, she was sure, a stripped one; it meant not collecting or possessing. She looked forward to *discovering* what was necessary. So far she'd accumulated a futon and an old portable black and white TV, the gift of Geoffrey's wife, Oenone.

'Geoffrey never has time to look at it and I'm not too keen on the content,' she said, apparently feeling that some explanation was needed for her generosity.

It was company, Theodora felt, as she wrestled with the Belling and a tin of beans, even though reception was not too strong owing to the cranes.

'Finally, tonight, the Archbishop of York today met the Archimandrite of Azbarnah at the headquarters of the Church of England, Ecclesia Place, Westminster. Our reporter, Archie Douglas, talks to us now . . .'

Theodora put her head round the door of the scullery and gazed towards the flickering image. She remembered Archie as a self-confident PPE man from Teddy Hall. He'd got a bit thicker ten years on but the confidence still clung to him like a halo. For his inter-

view from Westminster he was wearing designer battle
fatigues and a cravat into which was pushed like a
tiepin his tiny microphone. The Scottish accent which
at Oxford he'd cultivated had slipped away in the
course of time.

'. . . the Church of England . . . failure of its attempts
to reunite itself with either the Methodists or the
Roman Catholics is now looking around for allies from
amongst other branches of the Christian Church. Some
unkind souls might say that in reaching a concordat, as
they call it, with the Archimandrite of Azbarnah, they
are scraping the bottom of the barrel . . . an obscure
country of which we know little . . . a branch of
Orthodoxy midway between Greek and Bulgarian . . .
not clear what the C of E hopes to gain from the
relationship. What the Azbarnahis would get, on the
other hand, is fairly obvious. Stronger links with the
UK whether political, cultural, or even religious, may
help this economically backward country in its quest to
enter the Common Market. The Archimandrite, a politically controversial figure whose role under the former
communist regime of President Kursola was, to say the
least, equivocal . . . The Archbishop of York who signed
the pact from the Church of England's side told us   '

The picture panned to a shot of the Archbishop and
Archimandrite seated in the front hall of Ecclesia
Place. Theodora recognised the reception desk and
rubber plant in the background. The Archimandrite
looked well-protected by a bulletproof black robe and a
strong growth of beard. He sat very upright, his arms

29

folded, his legs crossed. He was rather younger than his title suggested but he had a physical presence and a stern, concentrated gaze. The Archbishop next to him was gazing steadily at a different camera with the expression of one who has never seen a TV camera before.

'Archbishop,' the reporter sprang up terrier-like at the tall figure of the cleric, 'can you tell us what the terms of the agreement with the Azbarnahi Church are?'

The Archbishop continued to gaze into the wrong camera. It showed his fine bony profile and strong triangular eyebrows.

He cleared his throat and said mildly, 'The Church prays constantly for the reunification of Christendom and for the mending of the broken vessel. This is particularly true of our sister churches so long in the wilderness of communist Europe. Our agreement today with our brothers in the Azbarnahi Orthodox Church is one small step towards that end.'

Theodora wondered whether he had heard the question. The vowels, the prose rhythms were those of a Cambridge scholar refined during a lifetime of prayer and theological debate. They made no contact with Archie's more robust concerns.

'Archbishop, I understand the Diet, the general assembly, the parliament, if you like, of the Church of England will have to confirm this concordat when it meets in a month's time. Will you be recommending them to do that?'

The Archbishop looked startled in an understated sort of way, as though this was a move of high politics which had escaped him. 'Oh, I think so. Yes.'

'Why?'

Clearly this wasn't in any script the Archbishop had been briefed with. 'Er, well, as I said, the benefits to both our communities.'

'Which benefits?'

'The healing of separation. The ecumenical venture,' he plucked from the air and then limped to a halt.

He's been told it would be a good idea but hasn't been told why, Theodora thought. The word 'ecumenical' usually stopped any opposition in debate within the Church; the Archbishop naturally felt it ought to do so outside it. He looked miffed.

Pity Archie doesn't know the hidden agenda, Theodora grinned at the face on the screen. The undeclared intention, presumably, was that if the C of E got in good with the Orthodox Church, if and when the Orthodox linked up with the Roman Catholics the C of E would be taken on board with them. Perhaps the Archbishop didn't think that way. Or perhaps he had never asked himself the more searching question as to why the linking of systems, bureaucracies, which sprang from such different soils as England and Eastern Europe without a linking of hearts and sympathies first, should be worth pursuing.

'Europe,' the Archbishop was saying desperately, 'our new or, perhaps I might say, our *re*newal of the idea of Christendom through the Common Market.'

Theodora blushed for him. She'd no idea she was supposed to have signed up to a particular political agenda when she'd joined the Church. Tough on all those Christians who had a different political stance. Really, had not bishops problems enough at home without pretending to be world figures with a political agenda? A bit of local shepherding wouldn't come amiss.

Archie seemed to think he had demonstrated the fatuity of Anglican thinking sufficiently. He turned towards the Archimandrite.

'Archimandrite, what do you hope to get out of this agreement?'

'Money,' said the Archimandrite, gazing unblinkingly into the right camera.

Even Archie was set back by such honesty. 'Money?'

'We need a big lot of money to fight holy war against infidel.'

'Infidel?'

It was rather nice to see Archie outclassed by this heavyweight, Theodora thought. Hadn't done his prep on this one.

'The Muslim. He beats our breasts, he hammers our gate, yes.'

Archie had had enough. 'Thank you, Archimandrite, thank you, Archbishop. This is Archie Douglas, *News at Ten*, returning you . . .'

Theodora took a moment to realise that the ringing sound proceeded from her own room and not the TV set. Where had the Archdeacon concealed his telephone?

'Hello,' said a voice she didn't recognise. 'Hello, is that Miss Braithwaite?'

Theodora conceded.

'My name's Tom Logg. You don't know me but we have a mutual contact, Nick Squires. We did a course together last year, "Gender Tension in Micro Institutions". He spoke very highly of you. I've got a problem and I wondered if I could come round and share it with you.' The voice was estuary English but pleasant though worried.

'How on earth did you get my number?'

'*Crockford* for your vicar, who then gave me yours.'

'It's rather late.'

'I'm in a fix. I really do need some specialist help.'

'Yes, of course. Come round. Do you know the way?'

'No. I'll be coming from Ecclesia Place.'

'Betterhouse Bridge and turn right or Albert Bridge and turn left. Keep to the river. St Sylvester's church spire unmistakable. Then left-handed at the British Sailor, right into Jenkins Wharf, Ferry Steps Lane and left into the Stowage. It's a cul-de-sac. I'm number one. The inhabited one, just. I'll leave the front door open.'

Tom was there in twenty-five minutes. He lashed his bike to the railings and stumbled up the unlit stairs to the flat.

Theodora rose from the floor to her full height of six foot one. Tom was about on a level. He shook her hand vigorously and sat down without further ado cross-legged on the floor.

'Very nice pad you've got here,' he said without irony. 'I do like the smell of Rentokil.'

Theodora warmed to him. 'It promises well,' she agreed. 'You said something about a problem.'

Tom paused, took out his organiser as though it was a snuffbox and tapped the keys. 'I've problematised it,' he said by way of explanation. He blinked at the tiny lighted screen, cleared his throat and embarked.

'One. I'm new in post as assistant to the CSD, Canon Clutch, working out of Ecclesia Place. Two. I was in charge of the arrangements for the visit of the Archimandrite and Archbishop of York this p.m. Three. An hour before the Archs arrived, I was checking the area around the conference room when I found a bishop.' Tom stopped.

Theodora raised an eyebrow. 'There would be lots about?' she hazarded.

'No, this one was out of place. I mean he shouldn't have been there. I mean he was dead.'

Theodora thought about this. She saw it might be inconvenient. 'They didn't mention it on *News at Ten*,' she said.

'Ah, you saw that. No, well, they wouldn't. You see, I hid the body.'

'What?'

'I lost my head. I couldn't think what to do. I mean it's not as though the training courses cater for things like this. There he was, dead as mutton, where he shouldn't have been. If I'd told the CSD we might have had to cancel the visit and then where would the C of E have been?'

Much where it had been for the last four hundred years, Theodora reflected. But it seemed unkind to say so to this troubled boy. 'So what did you do?'

'I rolled him in a carpet. Well, more a rug. You see, we've got the builders in. The room off the conference hall, the Turnbull Chamber, is full of decorators' clobber and bits of furniture. So I dragged him in there and rolled him in a rug and left him there.'

'Chancy,' said Theodora. 'What had you in mind to do with him?'

'In so far as I'd analysed the situation,' Tom answered, 'I reckoned I could put him back after the Archs left and find him again and then call the police.'

'Unwise,' Theodora opined, reviewing what she knew of police procedure and forensic medicine. 'So what stopped you?'

'The Archs were due to meet CSD at four for tea, then they were to go to the conference room with their support staff and do the final bit of talking, sign the concordat thing, and be all ready to go about seven. Interviews in the hall with the TV. All done and dusted by eight.'

'Well?'

'Well. For a start, the Archimandrite was late. We took the Archbishop down to the conference room and stood about a bit. Then he started wandering around, looking at the portraits and talking about his own time at the Place. Seems he was there twenty years ago when he was making a name for himself in Mission and Unity. He was making jokes about how easy it was to get lost in the place. Then he said something about "there used to be a short cut to the number two staircase via the Turnbull Chamber, which was very handy if you wanted to make the refectory ahead of the crowd for the tea break". Then he opened the adjoining door.'

'You mean, it was a door to the Turnbull Chamber where you'd stowed the body?'

Tom nodded.

'A nasty moment.'

'You can say that again. He went in and looked around. The staircase door was opposite him, and between him and it was a lot of builders' stuff, scaffold boards and paint tins and such like and also the roll of carpet.' Tom was sweating at the memory. 'I was right behind him, of course, but I couldn't think of any way of actually stopping him. I imagine rugger tackling an archbishop might be some sort of criminal offence.'

'Wouldn't be surprised,' Theodora agreed.

'Anyway, he was so near the rug he was practically tripping over it. He looked down at it and then he said something like "That's really rather fine, isn't it? Bukhara, wouldn't you say? When we were in Nepal we had a matching pair. I wonder what the pattern is."'

Tom stopped, gathered himself together. 'Then he unrolled the rug.'

Theodora was rather enjoying all this. 'And tipped out your body?'

'No.'

'No?'

'No body. Nothing. He took a corner of the rug and shook it out. Then he said, "It's a fine example of a tree of life. Look at all those animals and birds woven into the branches."' Tom trailed off.

'Then what?'

'The Archimandrite was announced and we all trooped back to the conference hall.'

'And afterwards?'

'As soon as they'd all gone and the coast was clear, about eight-thirty, I went back to the Turnbull Chamber to have a look. There was nothing there. I searched every room on the corridor and as many of the others as I could open. There wasn't a sign of a body anywhere.'

'And no one's reported a bishop missing?'

Tom shook his head. 'I don't know what on earth to do. I'm almost inclined to think I imagined the whole thing, only . . .'

'Only what?'

'When I went back to the Turnbull Chamber, I found this.' Tom fumbled in his pocket and extended his open palm to Theodora.

A plain silver cross about four inches by four inches glinted in the light of her single electric bulb. She took it up and examined it. It was a Byzantine cross, very heavy with a ring at the top which had been strained apart. It had no hallmark and looked in some indefinable way ancient.

'A pectoral cross,' said Theodora. 'His?'

'Yes. He had it on when I moved him.'

'You do realise,' Theodora said, 'that the easiest explanation for all this is that your body wasn't dead.' Indeed, it had not seemed to her from the start of Tom's tale that there was any other possibility.

'He was dead all right.' Tom was vehement. 'There was no pulse or breath and the eyes didn't move when I picked him up.'

It was the detail about the eyes which brought Theodora up short. Up to then it had been just an after-dinner tale, quite funny but not believable. Now as she imagined the unseeing open eyes of the dead man, she took hold of the reality.

'Have you any idea how he died?'

'You mean, was it natural or had someone killed him?'

'Quite.'

'When I first set eyes on the body, I assumed he'd had a heart attack or something. But if his body has been moved, concealed, wouldn't that suggest unnatural causes?'

'It might not. *You* moved him and concealed him but you didn't, presumably, kill him?' Theodora fixed the youth with her own honest eye.

Tom flushed. 'No, I didn't kill him. I was an absolute fool. I see that now. I lost my head. I shouldn't have touched him. I should just have rung the police and told Canon Clutch. But I couldn't face the pandemonium that would have caused.'

'So?'

'So I wonder what on earth to do. I can't go to Canon Clutch now. And I can't go to the police without a body. Naturally I thought of you.'

'Naturally?'

'Well, I know you know Ecclesia Place. I've seen you in the library there. You are clergy and know the systems. And Nick Squires seemed to think you were very . . . capable.'

Theodora sighed. She'd frequently suffered from this impression which she apparently engendered in the minds of total strangers. It was late. She was tired after her day's cleaning and decorating. She had to get up in time to serve for her vicar at the eight o'clock Mass in the morning at St Sylvester's.

'I suppose,' she said, 'we'd better go back to the Place and see what we can find.'

CHAPTER THREE

The Place

The bench outside Ecclesia Place was not much sought after. Maggie mostly had the patch to herself except in very fine weather. Certainly at night she could usually count on peace. As the midnight chimes of Big Ben came down the wind, she was able to spread her copies of the *Church Times* out on the bench to prevent the draught between the slats without having to share with anyone. Such freedom she counted a blessing. Indeed it was her chief reason for living (as she put it to herself) tough. She had parked her shopping trolley at the end she'd selected for her head and tied it with a length of dog lead to the bench. She took off her brown belted gaberdine and extracted from the trolley a bright red woollen pullover. This she put on as her nightgown and then put her gaberdine back on. She was vested.

She looked down at her feet for a moment to see

which way they were pointing and so get her bearings. Then she seated herself and ruminatively picked her teeth with a matchstick. The niceties of her toilette completed, she was ready to retire. She contemplated prayer. She'd been taught, as a child, to say, 'Matthew, Mark, Luke and John, bless the bed that I lie on.' But of late years, after, as she put it, her trouble, she noticed that if she prayed for this blessing, she was very rarely visited by the dream she most wanted. That dream was a dream of Eden. Her dream was detailed and greatly desirable. It comprised bright green fields and a very clear pebbly stream which she was able to gaze into while the sun warmed her back. Just out of her dream sight, there was someone who protected her. She never saw her but she knew she was there. It was a good dream, in fact, but in order to get it you had to pick your teeth first and then not pray. So tonight Maggie didn't. Instead she thought of her family. Today she'd invented an uncle to entertain old Jo and a nephew for young Tracy. She'd done the uncle before so she'd not had to invent so much; it was more a matter of pacing over old ground. But the nephew promised well; she'd rather liked the nephew, what she'd seen of him, and Tracy, poor kid, had taken to him. She'd invented a son once but sons were hard work. People expected you to know so much about them and you had to be consistent. They couldn't have red hair one minute and black the next. Keeping track of their ages was difficult too. And then people wanted to know why sons didn't come and help you out now and again. She'd always had to ship them off to Australia to stop them having to come to her aid. Sons tied you into the world, sons did. So in the end she'd stopped inventing them and stuck to nephews instead.

The breeze was getting up, she noticed. The plane tree which afforded shelter to the bench would protect her if rain came and it was a good deal cleaner and more spacious than dossing under the arches with drunks and madmen. 'Never got a moment's peace to yourself,' Maggie said aloud as she drifted, she hoped, towards Eden.

There were no street lamps immediately outside the side entrance to Ecclesia Place. So Theodora trod on the saucer of dog meat and milk left earlier by Maggie for her cats. Tom fumbled for keys and Theodora thought, what am I doing at five past midnight entering the heart of Anglican government to find the body of a missing, perhaps murdered, putative bishop? There were people paid to do this sort of thing. They were called police. Was this unknown young man's career so important that it should involve her losing a night's sleep?

'Do you know the Place well?' Tom inquired over his shoulder.

'Only bits of it. I easily get lost when I stray beyond the library or the refectory.'

'Good refectory,' Tom said. Nobly he put thoughts of hot sweet coffee and rounds of buttered toast from him. Since finding the body he'd not been able to eat. He was two meals behind.

'How about alarms?' Theodora asked as Tom put his shoulder to the door.

'If you enter with a key they don't go off.' Tom was reassuring.

The Church was evidently unable to imagine a mind so depraved that it would stoop to duplicating keys.

'What did he look like, your body, your bishop?' Theodora asked as they stumbled inside and closed the door behind them. They paused for a moment then Tom set off down the lightless corridor. Theodora felt rather than saw his tall back and followed close behind. After about twenty paces he halted and fumbled for the light. An ungenerous forty watts flickered into activity and illuminated a flight of what was evidently a back staircase. They set off to the first floor.

'Five foot six or seven. Barrel-chested. Strong growth of black hair flecked with grey and a beard neatly trimmed. Square hands, a bit rough round the edges, calloused skin. Perhaps a gardener.' Tom assigned a suitable hobby for an Anglican bishop.

'How old?'

'Late forties, early fifties perhaps.'

Theodora sensed that that was quite old in Tom's book.

'He smelt of something too,' Tom added. 'Camphor? Boot polish? Yes, that's it. He had a very nice pair of boots on.'

'Boots?' Theodora pictured the sort her father's gardener had sported in rural Oxfordshire: heavy black with an enormous tongue jutting out the top and strong laces which were, nevertheless, always breaking.

'Very smart pair of jodhpur boots or Chelsea boots, something like that. Brown.'

'Good gracious,' said Theodora, genuinely scandalised. 'With a clerical black suit?'

'S'right.'

Theodora, the product of eight generations of Anglican priests, reviewed the vast network of priestly cousins, uncles, friends of both, contemporaries at university and theological college, acquaintances from conferences and training sessions, and tried to bring into focus any of the forty-odd Anglican diocesan bishops who might fit the description. No one sprang to mind. 'Could he be a suffragan?'

'Could be. Or, who else has bishops?'

'Church of Wales, Church of Ireland, Church of Scotland, American Episcopalians, and what used to be called colonial bishops.'

'Oh heck,' said Tom. 'The place was awash with people yesterday.'

'Hang on a minute. What made you think he was an Anglican bishop?'

'The pectoral and the ring '

'What colour was his shirt?'

'Black. Oh, I see what you mean. It ought to have been purple for one of ours.'

'Right.'

'So either he was an RC one, which is unlikely, there weren't any on the guest list, or else an Azbarnahi.'

Tom groaned. 'I don't know which is worse, one of our lot dead or one of their lot.'

Theodora could think of no way to console him.

At the top of the stairs, Tom turned the light off, pushed through a swing door and turned right.

Theodora, who had a good sense of direction, was immediately lost. Tom paced confidently forward switching lights on at the beginning of corridors and off at the end of them. It was odd, Theodora reflected, that so orderly and methodical a boy should have lost his head in the matter of a dead bishop. On his present form he should have reached for his mobile phone and called the porters. Was panic all that had prevented him?

'What about times?' Theodora asked. 'When did you find the body exactly?'

'I had a late lunch, then I went to check the conference arrangements. It must have been about two-thirty.'

'And what did you do after you'd rolled him in the rug and stowed him in the Turnbull Chamber?'

'I came out of the Turnbull Chamber. I remember hesitating and deciding to go back to my own room. I wanted to think things out. But then I remembered that the quickest way to my room was up the staircase from the Turnbull Chamber and I really didn't fancy going through there again. So I was sort of havering when I saw the top of Canon Clutch's head coming up the main staircase.'

'Was he alone?'

'No, he had someone else with him. I only saw the top of his head but I think it was Canon Teape.'

'The Place archivist?'

'Right. Do you know him?'

'Our paths cross in the library from time to time. What did you do?'

'I didn't want to meet them head on, so I retreated back to the conference hall.'

'Which was empty?'

'Yes. No. Ashwood was there.'

'Doing what?'

'Moving in more chairs.'

'Where from?'

'There's a store behind the platform.'

'So at a rough estimate, at about the time you found the bishop dead, Clutch, Teape and Ashwood were all in the offing – as well, of course, as you.'

'Well, yes. But remember, the man must have been dead for a bit.'

'How warm did he feel?' Theodora asked clinically.

'Not very. I mean, it's difficult to tell. I was sweating so much myself.'

'But he wasn't cold, rigid?'

'No, he was sort of lukewarm and floppy,' Tom said.

Growth continues until death, Theodora thought irrelevantly as a remark of a medical acquaintance floated into her mind. 'Rigor sets in about half an hour after death depending on the ambient temperature,' she said.

'Which was warm. It's been a mild autumn and the

heating goes on on October the first regardless of need. It's one of the things they could really cut . . .' Tom trailed off.

The corridor terminated. They stepped out on to a landing which ran round the whole breadth of the building. Grey light filtered in smudgily from the glass dome overhead. Theodora leaned over the balustrade and gazed down at the flight of steps which met the landing about twenty yards away. She could just make out the marble of the ground-floor hall below. She tried to imagine it as it had been at three in the afternoon as Canon Clutch and Teape came up the steps and Tom retreated back into the conference hall. 'I've been here before, I think,' she said. 'But I wouldn't know how to get here unaided. Why is it such a difficult building to come to terms with?'

'It's asymmetrical. The site is really a trapezium. The difficulties for the architect were enormous, given that he had to make it impressive and still accommodate fifty-odd offices. They had a bomb here in forty-three which took out the north corner, which did nothing for the structure when they rebuilt after the war on too little money. The site was waterlogged too. You may have noticed the library and archives in the crypt are damp.'

'It does the manuscripts no good,' Theodora agreed.

'Originally the site belonged to the Archbishop of Canterbury and it had a Dominican house on it in the fourteenth century. Some of the underdrawing can still be seen. It was probably quite dry enough until they embanked the Thames in eighteen seventy. Then of course it disturbed the water levels and the old drainage couldn't cope.'

'How very knowledgeable of you,' said Theodora who knew all this.

'I took an optional unit in workplace environments with special reference to physical features influencing the dynamics of human interaction. Frankly, unless they blow the whole place up and start again, I doubt they'll ever get functional working practices in place. Too many individual offices and not enough seminar rooms. A sort of physical reflection of too many chiefs and not enough Indians. It affects working practices. Not enough interaction. Knocking a few walls down and partitioning some of the bigger offices, which is what the builders are currently at, is just tinkering.'

Theodora was impressed. Tom had categories for what she knew by instinct and observation. 'Have you tried your theories on cathedrals or parish churches?'

Tom shook his head.

'There's an interesting movement at the moment to try to deny what churches are for by reordering their interiors, making them matey, user-friendly, comfortable. The worst put in carpets and coffee bars, even the best tend to ignore the high altar. An air of apology clouds all.'

'That so?' Tom was interested. 'Might be a PhD there.'

Theodora looked at the two doorways to the conference hall and to the Turnbull Chamber. 'Come on,' she said. 'We're just putting off the evil hour.' They paced round the landing and pulled up outside the doors. The chair stood empty and solid below the theatrical bishop's portrait.

'Did you take the bishop, or whatever he was, to the rug or the rug to the bishop?'

'The first.' Tom moved towards the door to the Turnbull Chamber. They had spoken in hushed tones. Why? Theodora wondered. Was it the still lingering presence of death?

There was no sound from anywhere in the building as they stepped through the door. Once inside, however, there was a soft whirring and then a series of clunks and groans. Theodora recognised the sound of clerical central heating stirring into action, presumably controlled by thermostat. The room had no outside windows and only a smudge of light followed them through the open door. Theodora ran her hand down the panelling and pushed. There was a click and a flutter of purplish light from the two fluorescent bars in the ceiling. Theodora surveyed what looked like a builders' yard. Breeze blocks and mixing boards, open bags of sand and cement, ladders and paint tins covered the area. The rug, still partially unrolled from the Archbishop's handling, lay a little way into the room. They approached it cautiously in step. Theodora gazed at the tree of life which had earned the Archbishop's commendation. She knelt down and scrutinised it. She was aware how much more the police and forensic people would have been able to deduce than she.

'There's no trace of blood,' she said helplessly.

'I said, there was no wound.'

Theodora looked again. 'What there is, however, is cement, powdered cement.'

'So?'

Theodora indicated the layout of the room, the space from the door to the carpet. 'The floor is clean from the door to here. The spilt cement starts over there.' She gestured towards the torn bag spreading its powdery contents halfway down the room. 'Did you walk over there when you rolled him in the rug?'

'No. He was a dead weight. I had it in mind he'd be easier to retrieve if I didn't put him too far from the door.'

'And the Archbishop came in from there.' Theodora nodded towards the door on the left which led to the conference hall.

'Right.'

'And the door to stairway two?'

'Over there.' Tom indicated the third door in the room on the opposite side.

'So the Archbishop wouldn't have crossed the cement trail either. Or did he get as far as door three?'

Tom mimed thinking. He went to the left-hand door and paced from it, then bent over and held the rug. 'No, he didn't cross the trail. Handling the rug was the only thing he did in this room.'

'What about the rest of the party?'

Tom thought again. 'I was at his right hand. His chaplain was on the other side. There was a group of other clergy in the door who didn't actually come in.'

'And at that point the Archimandrite's lot came into the conference hall behind?'

'Right.'

Theodora got up carefully and made her way across the room. 'The cement must have come off the shoes of someone standing on the carpet who came across the trail from the third door.' She bent down again. Grey particles could be seen near the jamb of the door. 'He went through that door with, presumably, the body in tow.'

Tom nodded agreement.

'Which he dragged rather than carried,' Theodora said, opening the door and surveying the back staircase which fell away from them into darkness. 'Where does it lead?'

'Corridor at the back of the refectory.' Tom switched the lights off in the room, clicked on the staircase lights, and started down.

Halfway down there was another deposit of cement, small but unmistakable. At the bottom of the stairs they pulled up.

'Which way?'

Tom did his trick with the lights again, off behind and on in front. The corridor, narrower than those on the upper floors, stretched towards a fire door about twenty yards away. On their right were glass-paned doors through which could just be discerned the grills and counters of the refectory servery. Slowly, eyes on the floor, they edged down the corridor.

'Nothing,' said Tom.

They reached the fire door and Tom put his hand to the bar. He hesitated. Then he put his hand to the door itself. It opened quietly.

'He came this way then,' Theodora remarked, taking the inference in a moment.

'And had to leave it open,' Tom agreed.

Together they emerged on to the paving of the short alley at the end of which was the embankment court. Quickening pace, they strode past the paladins and more builders' clutter. Just before they emerged into the court, Theodora, whose eyes had not left the ground, touched Tom's elbow. She bent down and picked up a dark shape. She turned it over and then offered it to him.

'A brown leather boot, quality wear and nearly new. Come on.' He broke into a run. The lights of the embankment court made them blink. Tom raced ahead and reached the balustrade which marked the river. It came to his waist. He placed his arms on top and hitched himself up and peered down into the Thames. Theodora joined him. Twenty yards of undisturbed mud glittered and sucked and smelt under the cloudy sky. In the distance the shrunken stream of the river raced in a deep channel.

'Springs,' said Theodora. 'Very low tide.' She glanced downstream. A pleasure boat, lights blazing but no band playing, was gliding down the receding tideway. She felt a wave of tiredness as great as physical pain sweep over her. 'Nothing.'

'The Fatted Calf, tomorrow. Twelve fifteen. Yes?'

She nodded and turned upstream to Betterhouse Bridge.

Maggie watched as the two figures parted and went their separate ways. That was the second couple she'd seen emerging from Ecclesia Place tonight. Trade must be brisk in the Church for them to be working night shifts.

CHAPTER FOUR

The Foundation

' . . . Thy servant Elizabeth, our Queen, that under her we may be godly and quietly governed, and to all they that are put in authority under her that they may truly and indifferently administer justice to the punishment of wickedness and vice and the maintenance of Thy true religion and virtue.'

Theodora in her deacon's stall followed Geoffrey's quiet voice as he made his way through the eight o'clock Communion service in the parish church of St Sylvester Betterhouse. Tuesday was Prayer Book day and the congregation was Prayer Book: five very old women, two oldish men and one very young girl whom Geoffrey had recently prepared for confirmation. Geoffrey's wife, Oenone, Theodora noticed, was not present. Geoffrey, she knew, had hoped she might be drawn into the worshipping life of the church. But

Oenone had kept her teaching post at a smart independent girls' school in Kensington. She came to parish Mass on Sundays. Midweek church-going was alien to her; and probably inconvenient in its timing, Theodora had to admit to herself in all justice.

Theodora put thoughts of Oenone out of her mind. That way lay danger. After all, Geoffrey, she admitted, ran a good parish. He had had to build from nearly nothing and he did it by keeping his eye on well-defined goals. His naval training stood him in good stead. Worship, the offering of the sacraments and the example of the spiritual, prayerful life was his aim. Theodora discerned that he was without worldly ambition. He saw the Church as giving entry to a supernatural reality of supreme value, not as patching this world's politics or social services. Of course he prayed for the Queen's Majesty, for the state of Church and nation. But that did not mean he saw the Church as a political organisation. They prayed, she and Geoffrey, from a deep sense of England whose people had a right to their prayers.

They laboured towards their shared ends by visiting, by being flexible in the type of formal worship offered and assiduous in penetrating and nurturing the local networks. Prison visiting, hospital visiting, bereavement visiting, school visiting filled their days. Youth groups, wives' groups, childrens' groups were all organised and working. For her part, Theodora knew from her father what a well-run parish should look like. The small local good which lay to hand rather than the large universal good which was beyond reach was her goal. Quietly, unobtrusively, efficiently she performed her welcome duties. She made no fuss and no demands. She made lists and kept to them. She said her daily office as he did. If his marriage to Oenone had taken her by surprise, she reckoned she could cope with that.

The grand march of the liturgy pressed onwards. They prayed for those in trouble, sorrow, need, sickness or any other adversity. Theodora let her mind wander to the events of the recent past. This was a parish with plenty of adversity. And then there was the question of that other trouble, the death of an unknown man perhaps violently, perhaps a fellow Christian, perhaps a priest. What had gone on at Ecclesia Place yesterday while the prelates had been playing politics? What was it that Tom had stumbled upon?

Theodora glanced down at the small congregation. To her left she felt rather than saw the south door creaking open. She knew at once who had entered. A slight figure insinuated itself into the back pew in time for the prayer of consecration. Theodora kept her mind on the prayer and then at the end glanced up again. Anona Trice. Her thin androgynous face with its cap of red-gold hair glowed out of the uncertain light and, for a moment, Theodora felt a tremor of unease, fear almost, before she returned her attention to the liturgy. Perhaps Anona would disappear afterwards as unobtrusively as she had arrived. For no reason,

Theodora felt in her pocket and was comforted by the cold touch of the heavy silver cross resting there. Perhaps Gilbert Racy could help her with it.

In the vestry afterwards, Geoffrey, the fastest divester in the trade, paused at the door and turned back towards her.

'Oh, by the way, Oenone's having one or two people over from Ecclesia Place to meet parish types. Apparently she knows someone called Clutch. Big cheese at the Diet. Would you care to come and balance the table?'

'When?'

'Er, tonight, actually.' Geoffrey was embarrassed.

Theodora knew enough about Oenone to infer someone must have dropped out. She thought of the decorating she would rather be doing. 'Love to. Thanks. Time?'

'Good ho! Round eight.' Geoffrey departed at a working trot for his Lambretta. Theodora turned the key in the vestry door and made her way down the long aisle.

The church, the work of a single dedicated intelligence in the 1870s, was remarkable for its neo-Gothic exuberance. Angels with Pre-Raphaelite wings and ethereal facial expressions yearned out of the architraves of the pillars like a species of sacred topiary. What would Tom make of this as a working environment? Theodora wondered. At least there had been no attempt here to deny the purpose of the building or edit out the uncomfortable truths of Christian teaching. At the crossing was suspended Christ suffering. Behind the high altar He appeared again in majesty. Wherever the eye went, the iconography reminded the observer of the function of the place, worship, and the proper relation between man and God. It was at once luxurious and austere. It suited Theodora down to the ground.

'Good morning, Miss Braithwaite.' The voice interrupted her reflection.

Theodora jumped. From the shadow by the font at the west end, she recognised Anona Trice. A large head on a small body smiled up at her.

'Would you be in your new lodgings now?'

Anona didn't have an Irish accent but just occasionally the syntax of her utterance suggested the Celtic.

Theodora immediately felt threatened. She'd never wanted power but she did want privacy. She realised she had begun to think of her flat as her sanctuary, also her labour. The electrician was, with any luck, starting the rewiring this very hour. The last thing she wanted was that the Stowage should be seen, worse, visited, as though it was an extension of the Foundation of St Sylvester.

'It isn't quite habitable yet.'

'But you're living there, they tell me.'

Who the blazes would 'they' be? Theodora wondered. She and Anona had begun to pace down the path from the south door of the church through the vestigial churchyard towards the narrow windows and tall brick chimneys of the Foundation. The path was not quite wide enough to accommodate both of them. Theodora found herself walking on the verge. Anona turned towards her.

'It's down by the river, is it not? In the Stowage? That's a very picturesque part of the borough, don't you think so? I'd love to take a peep. A view of the Thames, now that's a romantic thing.'

Theodora thought, over my dead body. Anona trotted sideways along the gravel. Theodora was tall, Anona was short. It was not the only discrepancy.

'It's not really ready for entertaining in yet,' Theodora murmured.

'Oh, but I'm not needing entertainment. I'm as quiet, as silent as our friends here.' Anona gestured towards the graveyard's only tabletop tomb, 1870s with a canopy of defaced mourning angels crouching over it.

Anona Trice is not well, Theodora told herself. She was undergoing treatment at the Foundation. She'd been there on and off to Theodora's certain knowledge for close on a year. Theodora suspected, however, that even when Anona was well, whatever that state might be, she would have found her trying. She was importunate, foisting her emotions on you and seeking, requiring, a similar exaggerated response. She had a kind of anxious thirst. For what? For intimacy? For knowledge? For drama? Theodora feared it might be the last and if there wasn't one to hand, Anona would invent one. Anyway, Theodora found it exhausting, whether meeting it or resisting it. She set her face against it.

'Now you won't disappoint me, will you? You'll let

me see your little house? In my sorry state I don't get
much beyond a boat trip.'

Theodora had no idea what she meant by this last
and no wish to find out. She loathed whimsy and found
it difficult to be civil in the face of it. St Sylvester's
Foundation was mercifully within reach. The front
porch, in the style of a lych gate, reared up at the top of
a flight of steps.

'Is Dr Racy around this morning, do you happen to
know?'

'Ah, now there's a fine man, don't you think? Great
healing gifts. A really spiritual being, I'd say. Wouldn't
you?'

Hell's teeth, thought Theodora, why can't the woman
be simple?

'I'm sure you're right,' was all Theodora would allow
herself.

'Oh no, Miss Braithwaite, Theodora, I'm sure it's *you*
who are right.'

The tone, the abasement, the falsity made Theodora
squirm. The merely sad, the self-pitying even, she
could cope with, listen to, prompt until they were able
to listen to themselves, a first step on the way to self-
knowledge and therefore healing. But those who were
there before her and had self-knowledge enough to
play games stumped her. Which was why she'd decided
that, on the whole, she would make her contribution to
the Foundation by writing the definitive biography of
its founder Thomas Henry Newcome, who in 1861 had
sunk his fortune into building this retreat house of the

Society of St Sylvester for Anglican clergy and laity in the grounds of his friend Canon Langthorne's Church of St Sylvester. She had already made a preliminary survey of the sources and published in the *Church History Review*. When things were particularly dire in the parish, this secret work of hers consoled and refreshed her.

Theodora leaped up the front steps of the Foundation three at a time. She felt Anona drop away from her. In the entrance hall there was no one at the reception desk. She glanced at the sessions board. Dr Hertzog out, Rev'd Canon Butress in, Sr Hazel Millhaven in, Rev. Dr G. Racy in. Spot on. The house was warm, clean, newly decorated and carpeted. Gilbert's work on the boundaries of religion and psychiatry had recently attracted funding, especially from America, in a way that those in other areas of the Church's ministry envied. Gilbert might well arouse the mistrust of his more mundane clerical colleagues, but as a religious in the Society of St Sylvester there was little they could do about him. So he published his papers, saw his clients, organised the work of the Foundation and made sure that it catered for those distressed by their own or the world's evil. Groups were held, retreats given, instruction in the spiritual life, counselling for the bereaved and betrayed. Theodora reckoned they met a need and if Gilbert seemed occasionally eccentrically autocratic or even downright devious, it was, after all, *his* life's work.

The house was quiet. The smell of fried bacon

lingered in the air from breakfast, reminding Theodora that she hadn't had any. At the end of the first-floor corridor she paused and listened. She could hear Gilbert's high precise tones with the odd stress on the first word or syllable in a phrase which could identify him across many a committee room.

'*Of* course, I understand you. The *idea* that there are propositions which you understand and I do not is preposterous.'

Theodora recognised that Gilbert was on the phone. Priests were ruder over the phone than they would be face to face. She wasn't sure whether the same held for the laity. She thought probably not. It was one of the safety valves which the clergy allowed themselves. The fact that they were expected by the world, expected themselves, to behave better than anyone else meant that they had to let off steam somehow. Freed from eye contact, they let rip.

Gilbert was pressing on. 'I would not myself trust the Archimandrite of Azbarnah to sell me a second-hand bicycle let alone a . . .'

There was a pause.

'Well, all I can say is *caveat emptor*.'

Another pause.

'I would point out that it was you who sought my opinion.'

Theodora thought the moment had come to tap on the door.

'Ah, Theodora.' Gilbert replaced the handset and rose. He regretted all women so his manners were impeccably formal towards them. 'How very nice to see you so early.'

This was unfair since Theodora was punctual for every engagement and daily went to early Mass.

'I was not aware this was one of your days.'

'I come on *Monday* morning this term,' said Theodora patiently. Gilbert knew quite well when she came. He knew when everyone came, doctors, patients, kitchen and cleaning staff as well as the occasional helpers like herself. He knew what they did and how well they did it. And he made sure in his subterranean way that those on the staff who weren't any good didn't stay long. With clients, on the other hand, the feeling among his colleagues was that the more intractable, the more hopeless the case, the more likely they were to be made welcome, all possible care taken over them. Theodora thought that this was right too.

'The reason I looked in today is, I wondered if you could give me a spot of advice.'

Gilbert liked that. He relaxed enough to lean back in his chair and fold his long thin hands on his concave stomach. His domed head with its shadow of silver hair inclined in Theodora's direction. Theodora fumbled in her coat pocket and produced the silver cross from the missing body. She held it in the palm of her hand and extended it towards Gilbert. Gilbert liked guessing games which allowed him to show expertise. He took it and turned it over.

'A pectoral.'

'Is it?' Theodora was disingenuous.

'Byzantine design, of course. Silver not as pure as we have it in the West. The setting of the stone has been disturbed at some point and then mended.'

'What's the stone, do you know?'

'Belzique. Semi-precious. Popular around the Baltic in the ancient world. Easy to cut because soft when it first comes out of the rock, hardens later. Used for seals therefore. Not much mined beyond the seventeenth century. But of course there was enough in circulation by then to be fairly common. I rather like that dull bluish grey, don't you? Nicely understated.'

Theodora watched him turn it over in his hand. Gilbert, she suspected, had no possessions beyond a lot of books and a spare cassock. He lived, as he preached, on the minimum. But she could see he valued the cross.

'Yours, would it be?'

'Not exactly,' Theodora answered

'Got a provenance?'

Theodora had thought this one out in order to combine truth with as little information as possible. 'It got left behind after the Ecclesia Place junketings yesterday.'

'Ah.' Gilbert didn't sound as though he believed it. He tapped the strained ring at the top of the cross. 'Came adrift?'

'It does rather look like it, doesn't it? Could it be one of ours?'

'I wouldn't pretend to be an expert on the pectoral crosses of the Anglican Church,' Gilbert deprecated. 'But it certainly doesn't strike a chord with me at the moment. Anyway, whoever lost it will doubtless reclaim it. It must be worth five or six K at present prices. More to a collector.'

Theodora refrained from showing surprise. If Gilbert had said hundreds, it would have been more in her line of thinking.

'Are they much collected, would you know?'

'One or two in this country, more in America. Ecclesiastical silver is a *very* rich man's hobby. There's the scarcity of legitimate gleanings and then the effort of supplying provenances for the illegitimate. But there is the frisson of possessing something which has had a supernatural use. A cross worn next to the heart for generation after generation must, it is felt, have some special power.'

'Who would be a collector in this country?'

'Why? Thinking of selling it?' Gilbert was dry.

'No. I told you it's probably fallen off some bishop at yesterday's gathering. But if it came from one of the Azbarnahi entourage, it might be an easy way to find out if there was a Byzantine silver expert somewhere in the city.' It sounded lame even to Theodora.

'There's an exhibition of Azbarnahi art on at the Galaxy Gallery at the moment. You might learn something there. Though I'd have thought the Archimandrite himself would be the best source of information. If you can get hold of him.'

'I rather gathered you didn't trust the Archimandrite.'

'Listening to private conversations is not an attractive trait.'

'Gilbert, your door was open. You could be heard all down the corridor. Why don't you trust him?'

Gilbert chewed his teeth for a moment before answering. 'The rumour is, he did a deal with the communists under Kursola which involved his supporting Kursola's regime. In return he got the buildings and land and closure of the churches of the Roman Catholic minority in the country. The result was that the Catholic Church was left without a single centre of worship for half a million souls while the Azbarnah Orthodox Church mopped up the real estate.'

Theodora remembered Henry the Eighth. It really was no good Gilbert manifesting righteous indignation about ecclesiastical property deals. If the Church dabbled in politics then it should expect to lose some as well as win some.

'I'd better keep it safe then.' Theodora rose and swept it up from the table.

'Sure you wouldn't like me to keep it here?'

'I think it had better go back to Ecclesia Place or, failing that, the police.'

'Wouldn't trust them at all,' said Gilbert.

'Oh, and the Whip's Office rang, Canon.' The secretary was respectful and subduedly triumphant. She worked in the office of Ecclesia Place for the pleasure of being able to say things like that. 'They wanted to know if you'd like a debate on Social Responsibility. Housing was what they had in mind. They've got a space in the list after Christmas.'

Canon Clutch conjured up the bishop in the Lords whose job it would be to speak for the Church in the event of a debate. He focused on the evangelical fervour of Bishop Breezewell. The bishop had made enthusiasm a substitute for thought. It had carried him far in the Church. He was new on the bench and would need a lot of briefing to be even coherent, let alone commanding in his subject. It would mean a great deal of work for the Diet office.

'I think not quite yet. Ring them back, would you, Myfanhwy, and tell them the omens are not propitious.' Canon Clutch was roguish.

Mrs Gwynether drew a line through her list, with a flourish. She was a sloping woman. Her straight dark hair sloped straight down from her centre parting. Her shoulders sloped down from her neck, her bosom from her chest and her arms from her elbows. So when she rose, the impression was of someone overcoming gravity, of rising above the mundane into the upper air.

'And there's the Secretary of State's reply to yours of the twentieth of August.'

Canon Clutch took the thick creamy writing paper with the embossed portcullis at its head, positively his favourite paper, and scanned it. 'Regret pressure of business . . . unable to meet you . . . you do not say in your note what you wished to discuss with me. Perhaps you could put it on paper and let me . . .'

'Excellent.' Canon Clutch ran his finger over the portcullis to make sure it was embossed and not printed. 'Excellent,' he repeated, reassured of its bona fides. 'Put a memo in to Mr Logg. Tell him the Secretary of State has asked me to put together a paper for him on the housing problem. I shall want it by Friday.'

'Mr Logg's outside now. Would you like to see him? He's been hovering for ages.'

'I suppose I must.' Canon Clutch smiled a kind, colluding smile. 'We mustn't discourage youth, must we?'

As Tom replaced Mrs Gwynether, Canon Clutch allowed his smile to fade. The flesh of his large face came to rest on its bones as though the displacement had been accidental. He fixed his pale eyes on Tom. 'What is it now, Logg?'

He was beginning to wish he hadn't taken the youth on. He didn't seem to realise how very, very senior he, Canon Clutch, was. In fact he seemed to lack any conception of the fact that the clergy were quite, quite different from laymen, above them in authority, better in quality, superior in status. If that weren't so, there would be no conceivable reason for becoming one. He tried to remember Logg's letter of application. Methodist, was he, or Baptist or something that didn't count? Time, anyway, he put the boy right on one or two important distinctions.

Tom was not insensitive to nuances of tone, verbal niceties or subtleties of body language – he'd taken a course on the last. But he considered it unprofessional to allow them to dictate his own approach to work. He smiled his reassuring smile and drew out his perfectly typed, laser-printed memorandum in the text of which, Canon Clutch saw with distaste, were a couple of tables – pie charts did they call them?

'Look,' said Canon Clutch, hastily changing tack before Tom could get under way, 'I'm really rather pressed at the moment. In fact I'm absolutely up to my eyes. The diary . . .' he gestured.

'Just a couple of points,' Tom said jovially. 'I thought it might be useful to compare notes on the Azbarnahi operation.'

'What?' Canon Clutch was genuinely at a loss.

'Monitoring?' Tom nudged him. 'Review of past practice with a view to improving future. Yes?'

It was Canon Clutch's firm opinion that what was past was, mercifully, past. Learning from experience was not a strategy which claimed his attention. If things went badly, they were best forgotten as soon as maybe. If they'd gone well, and it was Canon Clutch's opinion that anything he was connected with went well, it would figure in edited, anecdotal form to entertain fellow diners at Brooks in due course. Beyond that there was no need to go.

'I hardly think it's necessary to pick over the corpses.' He stopped short, and focused his eyes suspiciously on Tom's open face. 'What had you in mind?'

'Review of systems for preparation of briefing papers, logistics of security and the handling of communications, TV in particular,' said Tom rapidly. 'The Archbishop could have been better briefed, don't you think? There are ways of not answering questions which can be very effective but not if you're looking into the wrong camera or don't understand the question or use bits of language which most people aren't going to latch on to. We'll probably need to think about rehearsal and prompt cards in future. So I thought that was a chance missed. The Archimandrite, on the other hand, didn't come across as all that user-friendly. Was it his lack of English which gave you a problem?'

Canon Clutch had had enough. 'You haven't understood. I am not prepared to discuss yesterday's events with my subordinates. These are highly sensitive, highly confidential matters which concern only the most senior clergy here.'

Tom was unperturbed. His obtuseness would carry him far. 'Oh, quite. Absolutely. I wouldn't want to compromise confidentiality. The detailed stuff of the discussion and the small print of the concordat naturally remain entirely in your and the Archbishop's hands,' he went on generously. 'No. It's the methods and systems that I think need a bit of tweaking. For example, my impression was that the security was a tad on the relaxed side. I had a look at Ashwood's records and it seemed to me there were more people in the building than actually appeared in his logbook. What do you feel?' Tom's tone was that of a professional conversing with a professional equal, genuinely interested in the articulation of alternative views, certain that reason, evidence and truth were the supporting scaffold of the interchange.

Canon Clutch didn't recognise the tone. He didn't want conversation with equals in knowledge. His staff were not his equals. They had only one function, to keep his in tray empty and ease his path with a measure of flattery and deference bordering on sub-servience. He was driven to desperate measures. He allowed his pencil to drop onto the table with a clatter. He leaned forward and brought the palm of his hand down onto the leather desktop. He raised his voice so that it carried to Myfannwy in the outer office. 'Don't you understand me? The matter is closed. I am not prepared to discuss it any further.'

Tom felt he wouldn't this time point out that it wasn't a matter of discussing further, they hadn't begun to discuss the main issues at all. However, he could make allowances with the best negotiators. 'Righty ho,' he said equably. 'I can meet you on that one. I expect you're right to allow a bit of time to let our ideas jell. We mustn't leave it too long, though, must we? Or we'll miss out on the detail. How about making a date for a meeting when you're not so rushed? Have you got a diary? Oh, and by the way, I wondered if you happened to know who sells good quality boots and shoes around here. I gather you're a bit of an expert.'

CHAPTER FIVE

The Fatted Calf

The Fatted Calf at noon was almost empty. Bright fake brass and deep-pile patterned carpets were waiting to reassure the influx of clerks and insurance men In another half hour. Inside the door on to Victoria Street the captain of the darts team, the Pharisees, drawn from the legal profession, was putting in a bit of practice before the rush. The Calf's main attraction was its forecourt which abutted Ecclesia Place's and ran down to the river.

Theodora judged it warm enough, this mild October day, to sit outside at the end of the court nearest the river. The urge to mark a patch, to set up a terminus, had been met by waist-high barrels of geraniums and busy lizzies posted at three-foot intervals. Beyond this, however, there was no attempt to keep people at bay. Tourists, pigeons and the odd dog wandered into the forecourt at will. Visitors were sucked in by the sight of others eating and drinking to pretend that it was still summer and set their drinks at the tiny uneven tables. The English were thawed, Theodora thought, by unexpected sunlight so that they melted and relaxed as though in the first stages of drink. Gestures were more expansive, voices slightly louder than they might have been from the scattering of patrons in the courtyard. No evil could be at hand in this grace note season.

Tom's arrival coincided with the first stroke of Big Ben. He had that look of ravenousness barely restrained by politeness which Theodora had seen on schoolboys still growing. He gave scholarly attention to the menu. Theodora drank pale sherry.

'So what have you learned?'

'The steak and kidney's quite good here or . . .'

She let him choose and order lunch before trying again.

'Learned? Yes, well. I've had quite a good morning in one way.' Tom carved his pie and amalgamated it with mashed potato and swede. 'Canon Clutch's not too hot on interpersonal skills, would you say?'

Theodora had seen Canon Clutch only once in Cambridge at a smart conference on 'The Church in the World: A Challenging Interface'. He'd chatted to a bunch of curates and then, when the bishops arrived, made it rather too obvious that he had better fish to fry.

'Difficult to work for?' she hazarded.

'Work's not really his thing.' Tom was judicious.

'He's a bit out of date too. Decision-making's very complex nowadays. You can't just go it alone issuing orders. You need to listen, consult and negotiate. Have good systems. Get the best advice.' Tom was well away. Theodora let her attention drift. It really was no good railing at people of the kind she suspected Canon Clutch to be. She had seen enough senior clergy of the Church of England to know that they were men whose talents entitled them to be humble. Hence they were drawn towards the political scene like puppies to the food dish, tails wagging, eyes glazed as they leaped 'to give a lead' or 'speak for the Church' on topics on which they had no mandate and about which they knew no more than the average layman. They mistook opportunity for authority. They were useless; they had soaked up the Church's resources and made it look silly in the eyes of the world but they weren't going to change now. In the end they weren't what Christianity was about. Best left, in her opinion. She tuned in to Tom's final utterance. 'Not too professional.' It was his ultimate censure.

'What about your corpse, your dead bishop or priest?'

'No one's reported anyone missing from last night's do as far as I've heard. No hue and cry.' Tom relished the words. 'But I had a look at Ashwood's record.'

'And?'

'Lots and lots of clergy. Three with funny names from the Azbarnahi end. Basilion, Polyeveski and Slynasiev. Nice curly foreign copperplate in Ashwood's book.'

'And what time did the Azbarnahi lot come?'

'Four-thirty, which is about right for when they got to the conference room. Ashwood showed them up.'

'What about our side?'

'Papworth had his chaplain, as I said. His name turned out to be Clutterford. And then the home team of Clutch, Teape and Truegrave. Only Truegrave didn't stay the course. He wasn't about after the thing was signed. Clutch stuck like a leech to Papworth and Teape trailed along behind, with the foreigners in tow.'

'Is Ashwood's record accurate?'

'No, I wouldn't think so for a minute. At least, his might be, but the lad was on for some of the time. What's his name? Teece? Trace? Kevin Trace. He's new and not at all clued up.'

'When was he on?'

'He took second lunch because we overlapped in the refectory round about two-thirty. So he must have been on duty between one and two.'

'Have you asked him?'

'Yes. "Did you see a bearded bishop about five foot seven in a bulletproof double-breasted clerical black suit with brown boots, Kevin, coming in round about two-thirty to three o'clock." "Who? Nah, don't think so."' Tom was quite a good mimic.

'So your man could have come in on the tide?'

Tom nodded.

'Where was the tide going to at that time, two-thirty to three? It would have been a bit early for the meeting of the Arches.'

'No. It was the first wave of the TV people.'

'Can't, what's his name, Trace, tell TV people from clergy?'

'I don't think he can tell one person over twenty from another.'

'So we're no wiser where or when your body came from.'

'There's just one odd thing. I thought I'd find out when the Azbarnahi party left, so I rang Brown's. The chap on the desk says that three returned at about eight o'clock in the evening and checked out immediately. They were accompanied by an Englishman who paid their bill.'

'Three? But I thought you said there were three supporters. What about the Archimandrite?'

'We don't know, or rather the hotel didn't know, which three it was. Maybe the Archimandrite was one of the three. But they took all the luggage from the four rooms.'

'Ought the hotel to have let them do that?'

'I got the impression they were glad to see them go.'

'What about the Englishman?'

'Truegrave, without a doubt, though not in uniform. He's quite unmistakable. Do you know him?'

Theodora shook her head. 'Never clapped eyes on him. So where does that leave us?'

'It leaves us with one of the Azbarnahi delegation adrift.'

'You think one of the supporters of the Archimandrite was your body?'

'Well, one little Azbarnahi didn't return home. And the body on the chair might well have been foreign.'

'Wouldn't they have noticed? Set up a hue and cry? Made inquiries if one of their number was lost?'

'Say they didn't know. Or say that Truegrave,' Tom deliberated, 'either knew where the lost one was, i.e. knew he was safe elsewhere, or knew he was dead.'

'You're saying that Truegrave may have been the one who moved your body? But why should he do that? Why, if he found him, not report him?'

Tom reached for the menu. 'I had a reason for not reporting the body. Maybe Truegrave had one as well.'

'What sort of reason?'

'Well . . .' Tom grinned. 'The treacle sponge is very good here.'

'I'll watch you.'

Theodora waited while Tom went for his treacle sponge. The pub was filling. A burst of Scottish-sounding male bonhomie, as impenetrable as Serbo-Croat, came from just outside the pub's door on to the terrace. She spotted a vaguely familiar figure distinguished by its short stature. It was Archie Douglas dressed as though about to depart on safari, in bleached linen and substantial boots. Left his pith helmet on the mock Victorian coat stand, doubtless, Theodora thought as she watched him exercise his professional talents. He swept the terrace with a glance to see if there was anyone present important enough to need his attention while at the same time carrying on the backslapping exchange with his two companions. For a fraction of a second he caught her eye and she read him like a computer screen. Could he place her? Then, was she worth the trouble of being resurrected? His question seemed to be answered by Tom's return. Archie swung his attention back to his immediate company. Tom looked very much the sort of youth who would have nothing for Archie.

'Look,' Theodora said, suddenly desolated by the ways of the world, 'dead priests aren't our worry. If we can get enough evidence together to show there really *was* someone in that chair, in the rug, and that someone, as well as you, removed him, then we could turn the whole thing over to the police and let them cope.' The dead bishop was fading from her like the Cheshire cat. He could be remembered, glimpsed, inferred only from his pectoral cross. As his reality diminished, she was left only with a wish on this pleasant day to be freed from the need to pursue him.

Tom poured cream over his pudding. 'I had a break,' he said casually, 'in the matter of boots. The CSD is frightfully knowledgeable sartorially. Tailors, shirt-makers, suits, that sort of thing.'

Theodora wondered if Tom supposed she needed to be told what 'sartorially' meant. Really the lad was obtuse. 'And boots and shoes too, presumably.'

'Right. Shotter and Cobb in Victoria Street. "Famous since seventeen ninety-three." Deeply rooted in our culture.' He paused. 'I took our one along.'

'And?'

'Well, it was all rather odd.' Tom plunged his long

wrists into his briefcase and extracted the boot. 'Notice anything?'

Theodora gazed at the beautiful tanned surface. Good for riding, she thought. Make a nice jodhpur boot. She shook her head. 'Not my area.'

Tom licked his spoon clean of treacle and tapped the handle against the heel. 'Listen.'

She saw what he meant. 'What would a priest, what would anyone want with boots with hollow heels?'

'Just what I asked the chap in the shop. Not so uncommon apparently. Travellers in foreign parts, thievish and uncivil countries, do sometimes put valuables, reserves of cash etc. in their heels. Gives a new meaning to well-heeled, yes?'

'Was this one of Shotter and Cobb's?'

'Oh yes. They aren't so vulgar as to put their name in them but there's no doubt they made it. He recognised it at once and it has a number on the inside of the instep.'

'And he knew whose it was?' Theodora waited.

'Made last month for Canon Teape.'

'The archivist?'

'The very same. Coffee?'

'Yes, thanks. Black, no sugar.'

While she waited, Theodora turned the boot over in her hands. The heel was of leather, hardly worn, fixed with five studs. She fished in her bag and brought out her Swiss knife. Carefully she turned the studs clockwise.

Tom lowered the tray onto the table. 'Clever of you to

spot it. Clockwise. I'd not have thought of that until the chap showed me.'

Theodora allowed the layer of leather to pivot on the single stud. The cavity was revealed. 'There's nothing in it.' She ran her finger round the edge of the empty space. A trace of white clung to her index finger. She smelt it, then cautiously licked it.

'What is it?'

'At a guess, I'd say chalk.'

'It's a lot of trouble to go to to carry chalk about.'

'Chalk would be quite a good medium for carrying something else about.'

'Drugs?'

'Perhaps. Though you'd need a chemist to do the separating afterwards. Also it's a very small space. You wouldn't make a lot out of drug-running on this scale. And it would be an easy scent for dogs to pick up, I'd have thought.'

'What then?'

Theodora thought of the Byzantine pectoral and the belzique stone. 'How about stones of some kind?'

'Diamonds?'

'We really do need to know more about the owner. Have you had a word with Teape? If this corpoc was wearing a set of boots made for Teape, the canon ought to know something about him.'

'He wasn't in this morning,' Tom admitted. 'Also I'm not sure what I'd ask him. "Have you lost a pair of boots recently?" Seems a little gauche.'

'Do you know if he normally wears boots?'

'Yesterday he was wearing an unexceptional pair of black shoes. I was walking behind him as we came down the stairs for the *Church Times* photocall.'

'I didn't know there was a *Church Times* photocall.'

'Neither did we. They don't count in Canon Clutch's book so we hadn't bothered to inform them. They'd learned through the national dailies that the Archimandrite was due and sent along a chap with a box Brownie. He lined them up in the entrance hall just before the TV people got to work. A marked contrast in equipment.'

Theodora thought of all the parts of the puzzle she couldn't see her way through. 'You don't think we could just go to the police with the boot and cross, explain about the body and let them take over?'

'No. Look, really. I'm sorry. I've simply got to keep my first job.' Tom was desperate. 'My career structure. I need two and a half years in this post. I simply can't . . . Also,' he admitted, 'my mother does rather depend . . .'

Theodora warmed to him. 'Right. In that case we need to be orderly.'

She took out a scuffed black Filofax and Tom reached into his breast pocket for his organiser.

'The problem is, one, the identity and provenance of the corpse. The only clues are the boots and the cross. With regard to the latter, Gilbert Racy told me – have I mentioned Gilbert?'

Tom looked intelligent as Theodora told him Gilbert's views.

'It does all rather point to the corpse being one of the

82

Azbarnahi party if the cross is Byzantine.'

'He also mentioned the Azbarnahi exhibition at the Galaxy. If the cross isn't Anglican but is Azbarnahi, would it be a good idea to look it over? Catalogues, that sort of thing?'

'If you do the boots and keep on with the cross, I'll pursue the exhibition.' Tom tapped a note into his organiser. 'What we also need to do is to find out the movements of as many people as we can around two-thirty at Ecclesia Place.'

'Given the state of the records as you've described them, that doesn't sound too possible as an enterprise. Why not just concentrate on Truegrave, Teape and Clutch? They were the ones most concerned with the Azbarnah delegation.'

'I'll do my best but I really don't have the nerve to question them properly. Perhaps I could get to them through Myfanwy, Clutch's secretary. She's a complete communications centre.'

'You do that.' Theodora rose to get on with the job. 'There is just one thing more. When I saw Gilbert this morning, he was talking on the phone either to or about someone involved with the Azbarnahis and the Archimandrite.' She repeated what she remembered of Gilbert's conversation.

'Could you ask him to clarify?'

'Gilbert, if he's that side out, would just refuse. Or else he'd want to know why I wanted to know.'

'Can we meet this evening and see how far we've got?'

'I'll be late. I'm dining at Geoffrey's. They've got Clutch coming.'

'Perhaps something will come out at your dinner party.' Was she mistaken or did Tom sound regretful that he wouldn't be eating that meal. She looked at the remains of the treacle sponge.

They walked together towards the embankment for a valedictory look at the river. Under the big plane tree at the far end of the court where the pub's tubs ceased and the undecorated flagstones of Ecclesia Place took over, a cloud of pigeons, startled into fearful flight, rose in the air. As they cleared, two figures seated on the bench came into view.

'The old girl in the gaberdine's a regular,' said Tom. 'The clergy find her difficult. She calls them all "Rev". She doesn't beg but they feel she's a reproach.'

Theodora understood. 'I've noticed. The poor are a difficulty for the higher clergy. They lose touch, not having parishes, and then feel guilty. Perhaps it's conversation, a not too demanding human contact, that she wants, not money.'

The pigeons began to settle again around the pair of women on the bench. The younger of the two tore up bits of bread into tiny pellets, breaking the bits with too much strength into the consistency of dough and then flinging them with a wild gesture into the heart of the flock. The older woman watched her maternally, turning her whole body towards her as though she might have something to learn from her actions.

'Hello, Maggie. How's things?'

'Lo, Rev.'

'I'm not a Rev.'

'All Revs at the Place.' Maggie was authoritative. Then, 'Got the time, dearie?' she asked Theodora in order to prolong the contact. 'That right?' she said as Theodora answered. 'Well I never. It's getting late these days.' She blew the crumbs off her brown gaberdine. Then, since that didn't dislodge them quite, she got up and dusted herself down. She looked at her feet to see they were still all right. The black gymn shoe on the left foot contrasted with the beautiful brown boot on the right foot.

Tom's eyes travelled downwards. 'Nice boot, Maggie. Where'd you get it?'

'My nephew give it me.'

'Didn't know you had a nephew, Maggie.'

He came vividly before her mind's eye. She'd had him, hadn't she, at least two days. 'He give it me,' she repeated, annoyed her word should be doubted.

'When?'

'Sometime.'

'Where?'

'Somewhere.'

'Where's somewhere?'

Maggie shook her head and gazed at the pigeons.

CHAPTER SIX

The Game

'The last shall be first and the first shall be last.'

Anona made it sound like a spell. She sat at her table in front of the window which looked out from the attic room at the top of the Foundation of St Sylvester. She could see over the rooftops to the river and the gables of Ecclesia Place downstream in the far distance. Big Ben had just struck noon. It was the right time for the game.

She opened the window and took a deep breath seven times. Then she turned back to the table. On it was a black and white chequered patchwork cloth. Next she took seven objects from various parts of the room and arranged them on the black hexagonals. She had assembled a key, a cross, a silver model of a crusader, a pebble, a small gilt flower, a thimble and a tiny candlestick. She folded her hands together and bowed to the bedecked cloth. Then she breathed in and out and keeping up the chant of the first last and the last first, she seated herself in front of the cloth and began to rock to and fro rattling dice in an egg cup. As the dice fell, she moved the pieces, seven throws for seven pieces.

Outside she could hear the hum of late-morning traffic and the odd keening of the seagulls coming up from the river. As the last dice fell in the seventh move, she adjusted her last piece, the crusader. She stopped and read the board. Her eye swept it from right to left. 'He comes not yet,' she said. 'He comes not yet. But he will come. He will return. I can't be left with nothing. There is design and pattern in the world. There is balance and harmony. That's what we've been taught. It's all a matter of reversal.'

Far below her she heard a door open and the sound of a group of people loosing from a session. She should have been there. Gilbert had said she mustn't miss any more sessions. But they couldn't turn her out. She was sure of that. A Christian house couldn't turn someone as sick as she was out on to the streets. And she a widow, or almost.

She was due to see Dr Hertzog this afternoon. She'd keep that appointment. She'd told them all, she was waiting. That was her career. She did it full time. It was just that others kept on interrupting her waiting. They didn't seem to realise how very demanding waiting was. It took all your energy. She hadn't time to do anything else. She remembered how often as a child her mother had told her to wait until she was grown up. So she'd waited, but she didn't know if she was grown up yet. How could one tell? When she'd married she'd done a lot of waiting. Wait until you start a family. But she'd waited in vain there. Wait till. Now she knew. Waiting was a thing in itself, a full-time occupation. If you started doing other things you fell between two stools, polluted the waiting. Waiting had to be pure. Those that wait upon the Lord shall be refreshed. The only way out of the waiting game was the power game. This game. She pushed the crusader back a hexagonal and then returned him to his original position.

She thought of the patchwork which lay outside the Foundation, the patchwork which was Betterhouse, then London, then England, then Europe. She could never get beyond Europe though she knew there was more. There was the world. But she couldn't get to the world. All was part of the game of power. The transformation game, Gilbert called it. 'The only reason I can't get it to work is that I lack the chief piece,' she had told Gilbert. But he had answered, 'The only reason you can't get it to work is you want pieces you can never have. You can only free yourself if you make the best of the pieces you have. That's how the healing comes.'

'I shall get him back,' she'd told him. 'No doubt of that.'

She placed her hand over the pieces and imagined them, the crusader and the key, looking up and seeing her hand hovering over them. Then she thought of the mighty hand of God above us all. She felt the constriction in her throat, the shallow breathing and panic rising within her. She had not heard the tap at the door.

Gilbert said quietly over her shoulder, 'It isn't like that, you know.'

She looked up into his pale eyes. 'How can you tell?'

Theodora, returning to her new flat after lunch with Tom at the Calf, was not surprised to find her front door kicked in. She regarded the splintered wood round the lock and the marks of the toecap at the bottom. Cautiously she pushed the door. It didn't feel like a door without its lock. It opened and she stood at the bottom of the steps listening. She'd cleaned the hall and stairs and sanded and Rentokiled the wood. But they remained uncarpeted. There was a faint smell of something other than Rentokil. Scent, was it, or aftershave? She mounted the steps to the first floor and remarked the door, which had no lock on it, standing open. There was no one inside.

Theodora knew the local talent would do her over. It was partly thievishness, which few in the area would see as wrong; partly, too, curiosity. What did this odd woman have? She'd given some thought to that problem. In the warfare which was endemic to Betterhouse, in which those who had nothing to do or who wanted money for a habit roved about like loose dogs seeking what they might devour, either you could fit a steel door and an alarm or you could simply own nothing worth stealing. She had never been able to formulate any argument which gave a convincing answer to the question, why is it wrong to steal? If you had what others wanted, what reason was there in religion why they should not have it? So she made her decision. She'd have no goods other than necessities; as little furniture as possible, no videos, no mobile phones. The food even was day to day. She'd lived like that as an undergraduate, as a young curate in East Africa. Why not continue so? It obviated worry.

She looked around. Whoever had visited had not been attracted by the ten-year-old black and white portable TV. The phone was still attached to its wires. The futon rolled up in the corner had been unrolled but not otherwise tampered with. She knew they didn't sleep on futons around here. The sun poured into the clean white space. The luxury, the necessity was books. The visitors had not touched anything from the shelves either side of the fireplace. Pedersen on Israel, Mowinckel on the Psalms, the Summa Theologica and the range of classical and philosophical texts stood in their places. Theodora's taste was for standard reference texts in the best scholarly editions; not a big market round here. She looked up at the ceiling. A thin pink line of new plaster ran from door switch to central fitment and the purple flex had gone. The electrician had come and done his work and departed. That would mean the robbers must have looked in over the lunch hour. Well, now they could put the word round the local pubs that she had nothing worth nicking.

St Sylvester's clock struck four. She checked her watch. She had a hospital visit to make, then some reading to do towards the confirmation class preparation, then supper with Geoffrey and Oenone. She'd better get a move on. She went into the kitchen lobby to take a final look. The teapot was safe. On the back of the kitchen door, her Barbour still hung where she had left it after Mass. She lifted it off its peg. Then a wave of physical panic swept over her. She drove her hand into each of the side pockets in turn. Nothing. She felt sick with apprehension. Frantically she went through the other four pockets inside. But she knew she was not mistaken. She'd left the cross in the right-hand outer pocket and it was gone.

Theodora hated blunders or muddles of any kind. She was organised for maximum effectiveness. It was part of the disciplined life she'd set herself on entering the Church's ministry. Nature, temperament had been perfected by training. How on earth could she have been so careless? The fact that neither she nor Tom knew whose the cross was made it worse. She felt she'd personally betrayed a trust. She reached for the phone. There was a delay.

Finally a Welsh voice said, 'Mr Logg is in conference at the moment. Can I take a message?'

'Just say Miss Braithwaite would like to contact him urgently.'

'Azbarnah, population estimated 1993, 5 million. Last

census 1952. The name of the country may be derived from the Greek 'Apbanikia', which is itself probably a transliteration of the original Doric. The terrain is largely mountainous with the highest peak, Mt Dovraki, six thousand feet above sea level. The inhabited part of the country lies to the north of the River Borka which is a tributary of the Danube. In Roman times Azbarnah escaped conquest by the Roman army led by Aflanius Agricola 97AD whose forces were led into a swamp north-west of the chief city of Vorasi and left there to drown with never a weapon drawn. Roman lack of success perhaps accounts for the description in Tacitus of the people as a *gens rudis et crudelis nec artibus nec scientiis imbuta*. The Byzantine empire sent its ambassadors in the time of Kropartoman the Small c.832AD, but they were able to do little more than negotiate a deal over copper mining rights. Later a type of Orthodox Christianity was introduced into the country by the Slavic saint Busonvici the Bearded whose miraculous powers attracted large numbers of the peasantry to him in the early thirteenth century.'

Tom, perusing the *Historical Atlas of the World* in the library of Ecclesia Place, turned the page of the large volume on its reading stand and tapped notes into his organiser.

'The economy in the classical and mediaeval era was founded for the most part on brigandage; the inhabitants were notorious for preying on the caravan trains which passed from the old Byzantine empire into southern Russia. The natives thus acquired a degree of luxury in the Middle Ages for which they had not paid a penny. In the nineteenth century the country escaped being annexed to the Austro-Hungarian Empire. Germany in the First World War did not think it worthwhile invading it. In the Second World War the Russians preferred to allow it to be governed by its own indigenous leaders with a form of communism which was scarcely more than titular and closely resembled the tribal- and family-dependent organisation of previous centuries.'

Tom gathered that the writer didn't think much of the Azbarnahis' social skills while evincing a reluctant admiration for their commercial talents. He ran his eye down the page. 'Although the country is not without natural resources, copper and tin, in the mountains, good building stone in the foothills and some timber on the lower slopes of the mountains, these have remained unexploited. On the whole the population has until comparatively modern times considered themselves traders, with a little farming as a basic economic stratum. The political organisation of the country has since the fifteenth century consisted of the *rakdomia*, an annual meeting of elected representatives of the main landowning families who after transacting the business of the state disperse once more to their own concerns. Hence Azbarnah has reached the modern era remarkably free of modern influences. In general it seems not too harsh to say that Azbarnahis have always managed to take what they wanted from foreigners while leaving themselves untouched though richer.'

Tom turned the pages of the *Atlas*, which was published in 1974, the latest edition owned by the library. The library of Ecclesia Place was buried below modern ground level. It was in fact a crypt. There were five stone arches with whitewashed bays between the bare stone ribs. Where the altar might have been, stood the librarian's desk, stacked with catalogues and half-empty mugs of coffee. The lighting was subdued, scarcely revealing the arcading of the roof. Libraries and churches have something in common, Tom reflected. They both sedate the raucous and unregenerate parts of us and demand a certain decorum. The silence was formidable. At five-thirty, it was not crowded. In fact Tom, cautiously rotating his head for fear of making a noise, could see only one figure, that of a small woman with a large head and small body padding slowly round the metal catwalks which stretched across the far ends of the library. These were reached by aesthetically satisfying spiral stairs. Every now and then he caught the gleam of the light on her fine reddish-gold hair as she reached down a volume. Of the archivist and librarian, Canon Teape, there was no sign.

'Find out what you can about Azbarnah and its Church,' Theodora had said, 'history and current state.' Tom had genuinely done his best but the gleanings had not been great. This was the third account of the history of Azbarnah from Bronze Age to Cold War which he'd skimmed. They all attested to the transport difficulties, the independence of the people (or their recalcitrance and rapacity depending on whether you admired brigandage or not), their freedom from outside influences. The standard reference texts on Orthodoxy traced Russian, Greek and Bulgarian strands of theological practice, the only clear doctrine being an undifferentiated hatred of Jews, Muslims and Roman Catholics. The strange thing was the lack of information about post-war development. There seemed to be nothing about how the country had fared under communism. What had they done for the last forty years?

Tom turned to the other works lying on his table. He tapped the title of the smallest of them with the date and publisher into his organiser: *The Cold War Frontiers and the Church*, ed. Ellis Bernhardt Truegrave, pub. Ecclesia Place Press 1990. A plate in the front indicated the volume was the gift of the author to the Ecclesia Place library. The contents page looked more hopeful than his last volume. Tom had all the intellectual curiosity of a youth with a non-specialist education. Those who had taught him at school had not been experts or scholars. The comprehensive system recruited where it could. Most of the humanities staff were geographers; the scientists had degrees in music and biology. But this had worked well as far as Tom was concerned. If it had deprived him of standards, it had also saved him from both fear and snobbery. Anyone could teach him about anything. Taste and see was his motto. He saw no reason why he shouldn't tackle and master anything. Getting down to a bit of ecclesiastical politics on the outer edges of Europe with no training in either discipline seemed to him a perfectly sensible procedure.

The book's contents were wide-ranging: 'Azbarnahi Geography and Climate: Barrier or Bridge?' by Etvan Groombridge; 'Politics and Policy in Cold War Azbarnahi,' Professor Ditch Molar, formerly of the British Council; a substantial article on mining's contribution to the economy of lower Azbarnah; an introduction by the editor and a concluding essay by him, 'The Enigma of Archimandrite Georgios XII'. That looked promising. Tom turned to page 277. There was a photograph of the Archimandrite in grainy black and white. The familiar features stared at at him. Tom recognised the corpse in the chair of Ecclesia Place.

CHAPTER SEVEN

The Vicarage

'*Te Deum Patrem colimus, te laudibus prosequimur, qui corpus cibo reficis, caelesti mentem gratia,*' Geoffrey intoned rapidly over the dinner table for the benefit of his clerical guests.

'I didn't know you were a Magdalen man,' Teape said as though discovering a rare volume on a forgotten shelf.

'Three happy years doing, I'm afraid, rather little.'

'Theology?' Canon Clutch inquired, hanging out his napkin like a flag.

'Physics with fencing,' Geoffrey admitted.

Oenone looked with pride upon her husband's dexterity with his escargots and garlic butter. Theodora, observing the dynamics of Geoffrey's table, thought how instantly men who did not know each other started in to form a club: I belong, you don't. But she caught herself up for being silly; a shared education is necessary to maintain a culture, a nation even. Naturally they would check each other out.

'Did you know Ralph Dunch, by any chance? He must have been about your time. He's just got his archdeaconry at Rabbitswold.' Clutch was indefatigable at mapping his territory.

'Geoffrey was in the Navy for ten years after Oxford before he entered the Church,' Oenone explained. 'So perhaps he's not as senior as he might otherwise be.'

It was, Theodora thought, the opening move in the game which Oenone, she did not doubt, would play until she got Geoffrey on to the bench of bishops. In a world which looked unstable, with its traditional institutions frail or corrupt, Oenone had at least the strength of knowing what she wanted. The present party was an early skirmish in that campaign. No one knows how bishops are made. There are no advertisements, no interviews, no one to whom you can apply. The criteria for choice are never debated in public. It is clear from the results that competence, whether construed as spirituality, pastoral skill or management prowess, is not the first requirement. Had Oenone chosen well in getting Clutch to her table? Theodora observed his expensive tailoring and understood how much he might dislike Tom, a nylon shirt man if ever there was one.

They were eating in what Theodora remembered as having been Geoffrey's study in the days when she'd had the curate's flat in the basement. It seemed

another life. Under Oenone's hand, and blessed with
her money, the Victorian vicarage had changed or,
perhaps, returned to its heyday splendour. Geoffrey's
bachelor establishment in which he had camped with
neat naval simplicity now looked and felt like a
gentleman's residence. Carpets new enough to sink
into had replaced the stained boards and slippery rugs
with holes in them. Chrysanthemums stood in a pool of
their own reflection on the sideboard. White painted
walls set off a couple of heavily framed oils, one an
architect's fantasy of St Sylvester's Church and the
other an impression of Ecclesia Place in the
apocalyptic manner of Piper. The degree of unreality in
both seemed to Theodora to capture things nicely.

Oenone had transformed the house. Had she also
remodeled Geoffrey? Theodora wondered. Had he put
on a bit of weight? Certainly he looked well He'd
shaved off his naval beard. His thick copper-coloured
hair gleamed with health. Marriage, then, agreed with
him, as it did with Oenone. She looked kempt,
accoutred perfectly for the occasion. She was dressed
('Theodora wanted to say 'robed') in some soft material
which it would be hard to put a name to, in a colour
midway between grey and brown. She was slightly
older than Theodora's own thirty-two years but looked
timelessly the hostess.

Theodora had been late; Oenone had led her into the
drawing room with a shade of impatience. Between
engagements Theodora had kept on trying to get hold
of Tom. The loss of the cross weighed on her like a

sickness. Where was it now? In some pawnbroker's a couple of boroughs away? Or had the thief known what he wanted and, indeed, come for what he knew he would find? She had had to put such cares behind her as Oenone made the introductions.

'Dr Racy, Gilbert, of course you know.'

Gilbert's eyes gleamed behind his rimless glasses. 'Theo, once again.'

'Canon Teape, Eric, archivist – sorry, *canon* archivist of Ecclesia Place.'

Canon Teape was well below Theodora's height. He pushed his grey face upwards in amiable greeting. Theodora could imagine him hunkered on a lily leaf in a pond.

'I think we have met.'

He blinked as though to take a better picture of her. 'But of course. Miss Braithwaite. The church historian. Newcome's biographer. Your excellent article in *CHR* for September 93 volume 37 number 4. A model of what such things should be.'

Clearly, in Teape's league she counted. And if she counted for Teape then she could see that Clutch was prepared to give her a trial.

'Miss Braithwaite, how do you do?' He stopped short and his *Crockford*-nurtured memory came into play. 'Not, by any chance, a relation of Nicholas Braithwaite?'

'My father.'

'I'm delighted to meet you,' said Canon Clutch with warmth. 'And so very sorry to hear of your father's untimely death.' Eight generations of Anglican priests, seventeenth- and nineteenth-century bishops, an earl's daughter for a grandmother, if he remembered rightly. Worth turning out for, just. And dinner promised well. Oenone, recognising her guests' needs, had shunted them speedily into the dining room.

'I very much enjoyed your letter in Thursday's *Times*.' Gilbert arched his long neck across the table like a swan seeking bits of bread from someone on the bank. They had swapped the escargots for pheasants which Geoffrey carved on the sideboard.

'I felt it needed saying,' Clutch assured him. 'The Church has a duty to give a lead at a national level.'

'I missed it.' Oenone shuffled plates neatly round her guests. 'What did you write about?'

'The Government's duty to house the homeless. It is quite scandalous. I look out of my window at Ecclesia Place every day and see a collection of poor people who need help.'

Geoffrey ceased his carving and applied himself to handing vegetables. 'We could do more ourselves. I mean, the Church could do more. The homeless are as much our responsibility as anyone else's.'

Clutch was prepared to be kind to a young tyro whose excellent food he was eating and whose connections he had not quite ascertained. He smiled forgivingly. 'No, no, you're quite wrong. That's not the point, is it? It's up to the Government. They have the responsibility and the financial clout to solve the problem. We, the Church, merely have the authority, the *moral* authority, to show politicians the proper priorities.'

'Surely we forfeit any moral authority we might have if we fail to follow up those priorities ourselves.' Geoffrey was very much the naval officer. He'd commanded his own ship. Men's lives had depended on his judgement. It made a difference. 'If we hadn't lost so much money by appointing incompetent financial servants – what was it they gambled away, eight hundred million? – we, the Church, might have done a bit more for the homeless. In this parish, we're trying to get a scheme going to help rehouse . . .'

Canon Clutch wasn't interested in the parish pump. 'At a national, indeed international, level – and we have to think in those terms, don't we – the macro economics make it absolutely essential to put a bomb under the Government. Some of us, those of us with clout, have a duty to show concern, compassion.'

A nice mixture of sanctimoniousness claiming moral high ground and power politics, Theodora thought. She glanced at Gilbert. He looked like a tennis aficionado at Wimbledon in a good singles match.

'We can't urge action on others and not take it ourselves,' Geoffrey began.

Oenone had a long line of hostesses in her ancestry. She had no intention of letting her dinner table become a shambles because priests didn't know how to behave.

'Gilbert, do tell us about your work at the Foundation. It really is a remarkable institution, isn't it? I hear you've done wonders for that poor woman, what's her name?' She turned to Theodora for help. 'Anona. Anona Trice. Geoffrey was saying she's becoming quite useful in the parish now that you've,' she hesitated over the term, 'stabilised her. And all without drugs too. Where does she come from?'

Gilbert smiled his Jesuitical smile. 'I'm afraid we never reveal the provenance of our clients. But yes, your kind words are, I think, justified for once. Mrs Trice is much better than when she first came to us.'

'*Mrs* Trice? Is she married?' Oenone attached significance to the state, Theodora realised. Was it because she had married late herself or because she hadn't expected to marry?

'Trice is her maiden name,' said Gilbert. 'The "Mrs" designates her marital status.'

Oenone looked as if she were none the wiser

'Oh, come along, Gilbert, don't make such a mystery of things. We all know who she's married to.' Teape's tone was not quite comradely. He didn't like Gilbert, Theodora inferred.

'I think it's better to respect the client's wishes.' Gilbert's voice was high and slightly nasal, snake-like, in tone. It stopped Teape in his tracks. Theodora thought how quickly the senior clergy pull out the card of moral superiority. In this case, though, perhaps Gilbert had a point.

'I suppose American money comes in very handy?' Clutch was smiling at Gilbert.

'I wouldn't for a moment deny it.'

'And American methods, therapy via games playing,' Geoffrey invited.

'The ludic element is very important and largely lost from our mainstream therapies.'

'But dangerous?' Geoffrey pressed him.

'We think we know what we're doing and without the research we couldn't claim the money. As it is we've been able to double our provision for clients over the last three years. We can publish more and all of us do. We are, I think I may say,' Gilbert leaned forward towards Clutch, 'at the cutting edge of the Church's contribution to the psychological sciences.'

Theodora thought 'cutting edge' was a bit of Clutch diction, and if Gilbert's 'ludic element' was just research fodder to push back the boundaries of knowledge, she only hoped he was right when he said he knew what he was doing with Anona.

'I'd have thought that that was a bit of a dead end.' Clutch's vowels got plummier as he got more annoyed. 'The Church has managed quite well for two thousand years without this bogus fiddle faddle.'

'Unless the Church can heal the sick, especially the sick of mind, it is not fulfilling its apostolic role.'

'It's the National Health's job to—'

'But surely, Gilbert,' Theodora was drawn in in spite of herself, 'we can only heal ourselves. There is nothing anyone can do *for* us, *instead of* us. We have to carve our own path to safety.'

'There is always grace.' Geoffrey was willing to have a go if the argument was going to get theological.

'But the whole point of grace is that we dare not *predict* it. We have to do the work first.' Theodora found herself more disturbed than she meant to allow herself to be. She felt that Anona's safety, Anona (whom she did not like), Anona's sanity was perhaps in the hands of these mistaken, experimental, possibly manipulative people. 'What the Church needs,' she fixed Gilbert with an accusatory eye, 'is to see how the traditional Catholic religious practices, prayer, silence, meditation on scripture, use of sacrament and liturgy, can meet the psychological needs of the sick. Then—'

'How about Ecclesia Place, Canon Clutch?' Oenone had had enough. She distrusted psychology; she did not understand religion. She didn't really see how these two could fit together and wondered how anyone could take either seriously. She had more important political or at least social ends in view. She judged it was time to allow Clutch to dominate the table again. 'You really must have a bird's eye view of affairs there.'

Clutch rose to the occasion. 'It's really enormously rewarding work, as you can imagine. Terribly interesting. The buzz. The hum. Of course we're right at the centre, the very heart of Government.'

'Who do you report to?' Gilbert was disingenuous. No man was more knowledgeable about Church systems than Gilbert.

'I am answerable to a committee of ninety-three members. Most of them are very busy bishops and immensely senior civil servants widely dispersed over this country and others. It meets twice a year for a couple of hours. Few comprehend the standing orders let alone the intricacies of the business. They trust me implicitly.'

Theodora wondered who was more dangerous, the incompetent committee or the hubristic canon. Really, if the Church couldn't get its own systems right, how could it tell others, the Government for example, how to run theirs? She thought again of Tom Logg and how he would have dived into this particular argument.

'But then of course there is the Diet,' Canon Clutch went on with distaste. His duties with regard to the democratic processes of Church government were clearly bitter in his mouth. Not a democrat, Theodora thought. She searched her memory to recall how the Diet worked. 'Keep off committees,' her father had said to her when she was deaconed, speaking from his wealth of parish experience. 'The proper work of the Church in the world is done in parishes, cathedrals, the religious orders and church schools. Anywhere else is a waste of energy and money.' It was almost the only piece of practical clerical advice he had offered her before his death. She wondered how her father would have got on with Geoffrey. Rather well, probably. And with Oenone? Well, he'd liked handsome, intelligent women, and he hadn't judged them by quite the same criteria as he judged men.

'Kenneth keeps everything in his own hands,' Canon Teape croaked, raising his eyes from his plate to which he'd been giving full attention. Theodora couldn't quite place his tone. Was it admiring or derisory?

'I have one of the best teams in the country.' Clutch patted him metaphorically on the head. So it was admiration, or at least Clutch took it to be such. 'Of course, our responsibilities are enormous. Quite enormous.' Canon Clutch shook his head at their mammoth extent. 'Our advisory role is crucial. People, the Government, look to us to give a lead. Sometimes, when you have real power, you have to take very hard decisions, very hard ones indeed. Then you have to have faith that the end justifies the means.'

Did this man realise what he was saying? Theodora wondered. How could he so complacently invoke that arch slogan of moral corruption down the ages which it was the duty of religion always and everywhere to combat?

'Don't you need a lot of expertise, I mean specialist knowledge which has nothing to do with religion to sustain that sort of level of political involvement?' Geoffrey was such a dear, Theodora thought. She wouldn't have had the courage to take on the appalling Clutch herself.

'We have it, I promise you.' Clutch was immensely reassuring. 'There is no sphere of political or social life where the Church cannot call on the very best specialist advice.'

'Pity we don't follow it then.' Gilbert was acid. 'Or is that because expert advice very often contradicts it-self?'

'Or better still, stick to our lasts and teach people

how to pray.' Geoffrey wasn't going to leave well alone in spite of the furrowing of his wife's brow.

'Made a bit of a pig's ear of your publicity for the Azbarnah thing, didn't you?' Gilbert returned to the fray.

Gilbert didn't care, didn't have to care what Canon Clutch thought of him. Gilbert wasn't a parish priest seeking preferment. He didn't have to take account of either diocese or Diet. It gave him freedom, it made him unpopular. He couldn't have cared less. He was sub-warden of the Society of St Sylvester, a religious, bound by his vows to its rule which, as Theodora well knew from her researches into the life of Newcome, was dedicated to the maintenance of the Catholic tradition within the Church of England. Really, Theodora thought, looking round the table and drinking Oenone's Margaux with pleasure, we have the Church of England's diverse elements gathered here. And how diverse they are, how different from each other in aims and methods: an honest parish priest, an ambitious politician, a scholar, a religious and a woman in deacon's orders. Her spirits rose with the excellence of the wine and her sharpened perception of the ritualised and theatrical on which a dinner party depends. She was beginning to enjoy the fray. What a blessing it was that she had no wish to rise up the hierarchy.

'Azbarnah is such an interesting country,' Oenone was saying, scenting danger to Canon Clutch's ego and therefore willing to protect her most important guest.

'One of my uncles spent some time there in the sixties as military attaché in Vorasi, when Kursola was in power. I remember him saying how beautiful the country was and how brutal the ruling classes were.'

'Archie Douglas hadn't done his prep, had he?' Gilbert was unwilling to be ridden off his promising new ground of dispute. 'That old pirate the Archimandrite ran rings round him. What on earth did Papworth think he was doing? Who on earth advised him? It really doesn't matter whether we're in communion with Azbarnahi Orthodoxy or not. No single soul in either Church will be saved by such an alliance.' Gilbert didn't care what his hostess wanted. Protection of Kenneth Clutch's self-importance wasn't one of his priorities. 'Anyway,' he concluded in triumph, 'Diet will have to ratify and they may have a rush of common sense and vote it down.'

'You knew Archie at Oxford, didn't you?'

It was a measure of Oenone's desperation that she looked to Theodora. It was no good. Clutch wasn't to be diverted.

'The media,' said Canon Clutch reverently, 'are terribly important. And I can't agree with you, Gilbert,' the tone was both comradely and patronising, 'about the Azbarnahi Orthodox Church. Of course Papworth scarcely begins to comprehend the political ramifications. That's not the function of archbishops.' He laughed to show how he forgave them their limitations. 'However I am myself monitoring affairs there very carefully.'

111

So that makes it all right then, Theodora thought. She was surprised by Gilbert's venom and his persistence. Was it directed against the Azbarnahis or against Clutch?

'Cheese,' said Oenone valiantly. 'Theo, I wonder if . . .' Theodora rose and followed her out of the room. Oenone ran a hand across her brow. 'Do clergy usually behave as badly as this?'

'I have known it,' Theodora admitted. 'Though I think Clutch is a fairly extreme example.'

'I wasn't thinking of Clutch so much as Gilbert. I'd no idea he felt as he does. Are he and Clutch personal enemies?'

'If they weren't before, they will be now, wouldn't you say?'

'I always thought Gilbert was rather reserved and mannerly.'

Theodora could only wonder at someone who could interpret Gilbert's intention to have every human encounter on his own terms as either reserved or mannerly. 'Greek meets Greek.'

Oenone was grim. 'Who carries more clout?' she asked, an amateur to a professional.

'In the Church? It's an interesting question. It depends what you're after. For certain sorts of living in the Catholic tradition, Gilbert. I think Clutch may have more pull in the evangelical area.'

'Who's in control at the moment?'

'Evangelicals.'

'Right,' said Oenone. Her tone indicated she'd made

her decision. Clutch it would have to be. 'God, it's all so complicated,' Oenone complained. 'I was brought up among soldiers who are paragons of simplicity and rectitude compared with this lot.'

Theodora was sure she had a point. 'Do you want both the Stilton and the Brie?'

'Yes, if you don't mind. The Brie's a bit overripe.' Oenone sorted the plates in what Theodora remembered had been her and Geoffrey's joint kitchen in former days. Oenone had redone it in accordance with the best modern taste; stripped pine was everywhere.

'Did you say Truegrave was looking in?'

'I hope to God he comes soon.'

They were halfway across the hall when the front doorbell rang.

CHAPTER EIGHT

The Dinner

Canon Truegrave was a hairy man, not in the sense that he had a lot of hair on his head – there, indeed, the growth was sparse. But what there was of it, widely dispersed across his cranium, had great presence, due perhaps to its quality which was that of strong grey wire. On other areas of his person, in the ears and nostrils, for example, hair sprouted out in greater and softer abundance. Over the back of his hands, curly black bristles disappeared up his cuffs leading, as it were, the eye of imagination upwards to speculate about whither the growth extended and finished. Was he hirsute all over? He wore a wide clerical collar which stood out at some distance from his raddled and none too clean neck. In one ear, Theodora noticed, there nestled a hearing aid.

'How's the old high Slavonic coming along,

Bernhardt?' Gilbert leaned across the table and addressed the hearing aid. Old friends or old enemies? Theodora wondered as she helped Geoffrey to carve and then hand a plate of pheasant while Oenone saw about the wine.

Truegrave gazed at the plate in wonder. Were they really offering him food? 'Thank you, thank you, yes, yes, certainly a little more. A leg would be most acceptable. Old high Slavonic is not an easy language,' he said severely to Gilbert, who nodded in sympathy as though beating time to a tune he knew well. Canon Truegrave chewed rapidly along the leg, which he held in one hand over the plate and brought his jaws to engage with by leaning forward.

'But it's very necessary, isn't it, Bernhardt, to be able to communicate with the Azbarnahis?' Teape tried the other, the non-hearing-aid ear. 'Their liturgy is in it, isn't it?'

'Thank you, potatoes would be very welcome,' responded Truegrave.

Theodora glanced across at Oenone in sympathy. Would she lose her nerve?

But Oenone was made of sterner stuff. If Canon Truegrave was an eater, and he was clearly that, she'd make sure his needs were catered for. Gravy, beans, carrots, redcurrant jelly, all were marshalled in the canon's part of the table. He did not, Theodora noticed, bother with a napkin in its normal prophylactic function, using it rather at the conclusion of operations in the manner of a bath towel to scrub his lips, the front of his jacket and the surrounding table. There was a palpable sigh of relief from the rest of the diners as he concluded his course.

'Cheese?' Oenone inquired.

Canon Clutch took the precaution of cutting more of the Brie before releasing it in Truegrave's direction. Possibly Clutch had dined with Truegrave before. The table abandoned any attempt at conversation and gave itself up to the spectator sport of gazing fascinated as Truegrave worked through the Brie, looked round for Stilton, was passed Stilton and looked round for biscuits. Finally, running his index finger round the back of his teeth, he leaned back in his chair, tapped the hearing aid back into place (perhaps it had worked loose in the course of his exertions) and appeared to change gear for conversation. Obviously a man who did one thing at a time, Theodora concluded.

'How did you come to miss the photocall for the *Church Times* on Monday after the meeting with the Archimandrite?' Theodora's question was unexpected to the rest of the table and drew every eye to her. But Truegrave took it in his stride.

'A lot of clearing up to do. Concordats make for work. Not that there are that many of them,' Canon Truegrave admitted.

'And what brought us to make this one?' Geoffrey had caught Theodora's interest.

Canon Teape sniggered. 'Bernhardt's interest in old high Slavonic.'

'It's the most enormously important political step,' Canon Clutch began.

Canon Truegrave either hadn't heard them or didn't care. 'I've known Mikel since the old days of Kursola.' Canon Truegrave seemed to think that this sufficiently explained why the whole of the Anglican Church should be committed to entering into theological and financial relations with a branch of Orthodoxy of which little was known.

'Mikel?' Oenone was the one who had no Church background. 'I thought he was called Georgios.'

'He took Georgios as his ecclesiastical name when he was put in.' Truegrave seemed happy to talk about the topic. 'I knew the whole family,' he pressed on. 'His grandfather had a lot of land in the Northern Province.'

'A landowning family?' Geoffrey asked.

'Oh, enormous, and branches in commerce in the south.'

'But communism?'

'Not quite the orthodox Marxist-Leninist kind.'

'You mean it never did away with private property?'

'Does any regime, ever? Just shuffles it about a bit, in my experience. Though in the case of the Turannidi family they managed to shuffle it about among themselves.' Canon Truegrave seemed to find that admirable.

'And the Church?'

'Ah, the Orthodox Church has some marvellous stuff. Almost untouched by outside influences.

Tremendously patriarchal but none the worse for that.'

Theodora saw that Clutch agreed that that was all right too.

'The landed families provide the priests as well as the generals. The Turannidi have had the Archimandrite's office now for six or seven generations.' This clearly made it all right. Theodora was beginning to feel glad she didn't live in Azbarnah.

'You've spent a lot of time there, haven't you, Bernhardt?' Canon Teape's tone was again opaque to Theodora. Was he setting Truegrave up or genuinely admiring?

'Lots of contact.' Truegrave was complacent.

'What happened to that chap who used to come and stay with you?' It was Gilbert this time.

Canon Truegrave looked vague, 'So many of them. Nephews of Mikel. One or two research students from the university at Vorasi. I give what help I can.'

'I never know where you stack them, Bernhardt,' Canon Teape pressed on, 'in that tiny flat of yours.'

'Bernhardt has a flat under the flight path for Terminal Two at Heathrow,' Canon Clutch was jocular, 'so he can depart for foreign parts at a moment's notice.'

'Always keep a bag packed,' Canon Truegrave agreed.

'Fruit? Dessert?' Oenone seemed to have recovered enough from the spectacle of Truegrave's assault on the previous courses to venture further down the menu.

Canon Truegrave perked up. 'Fruit,' he said hungrily. 'Dessert. How very welcome.'

'What were his boots like?' Tom turned the single malt in his hand and pushed his back against the packing case on which the TV rested in the flat in the Stowage. St Sylvester's clock had struck midnight. He'd paced up and down the Stowage for an hour waiting for Theodora to return from Geoffrey's dinner party. They'd slid up the stairs almost surreptitiously.

'Interesting you should ask that. He was badly turned out. Suit not of the cleanest, collar could do with a sponge-over but Canon Teape's boots were good enough to have come from . . .'

'Shotter and Cobb?'

'Right. But there is just one thing. The boots we found were what size?' Theodora asked.

'Biggish, say size ten.'

'Canon Teape's feet, on the other hand, looked to me smallish, say six or sevens.'

'So the ones we found must have been specially made to Teape's orders but for the corpse.'

'Looks like it,' Theodora agreed.

'How usual is it for clergy to wear boots?' Tom asked.

'I had a cousin who rode to hounds and wore them to early service under a cassock – without spurs of course. But those were long boots not short ones like these. I'd have thought it quite rare.'

'You did ask him where he had them made, didn't you?'

'I really felt I couldn't do that to Oenone. It was all quite fraught enough. Clutch and Gilbert had a spat early on. Then Geoffrey and Clutch had a run-in. Then Truegrave attacked the food as though fresh from a gulag. Furthering Geoffrey's career is going to be a tiresome business.'

'Odd to use a meal to further a career,' Tom commented. 'Eating is for eating.'

'Not in Oenone's world. Or Canon Clutch's either, I wouldn't have thought.'

'But you did learn that Canon Truegrave has contacts with the Archimandrite's family, the Turannidi. And, as I said, the photograph in Truegrave's book is of the body on the chair not of the chap who signed the concordat and appeared on telly.'

Theodora poured herself more coffee and thought how much she liked Tom. He'd passed no word of blame for the loss of the cross, had waited until she'd got coffee and kicked her shoes off before either questioning her or offering her his own new intelligence. She considered his self-control admirable, given what the top brass had thought it allowable to do in the previous three hours.

'What are the possible permutations?'

Tom reached for his organiser and clearly felt happier with it in his hand. He tapped in the equation, 'X equals the true Archimandrite'.

Theodora watched with interest then continued, 'The man who signed the concordat is really the Archimandrite but the photographer in the book made a mistake or the photograph is wrongly captioned. Or . . .'

'Or . . .' Tom took up the tale from his organiser, 'the photograph is right and the corpse is the true Archimandrite and the concordat signer is the false Archimandrite.'

'When did Truegrave meet the Archimandrite on Monday? Was it when he first came at four o'clock?'

'I assume so. I mean the Archimandrite flew in on Sunday night, according to the schedule I was given by Clutch. I don't think Truegrave had an appointment before that.'

'But Truegrave knew the Archimandrite well. He said so this evening.'

Tom was baffled. 'So if he met the false Archimandrite over the conference table he ought to have known it wasn't him.'

'Unless, as I said, the photograph was a mistake or wrongly captioned.'

'Or unless Truegrave wasn't surprised.' Tom completed his equation.

'Meaning?'

'Truegrave and the false Archimandrite are in collusion.'

'Over what?'

'Over the corpse of the putative Archimandrite and his boots with hollow heels.' Tom looked at his organiser as though he didn't want to believe it. 'Have we got all the variables?'

'Quite enough for the moment.' Theodora was firm.

'So we need to know the movements of Truegrave
well prior to the concordat meeting, say from Sunday
evening onwards, as well as the movements of Teape
and Clutch just before the meeting. It would also be
helpful to be a bit clearer about the degree of relationship between Truegrave and the Archimandrite, the
true one and the false one.'

'And what Truegrave did after the concordat meeting. Do I gather you think Teape, Clutch and
Papworth stayed together all the time from the close
of the meeting until the photocall and the TV interview but that Truegrave disappeared soon after the
meeting?'

'Right. Someone besides me moved the body between
three and the Archbishop poking around in the carpet
at four. And they had to have a reason and they had to
have an opportunity.'

'I think you mentioned Canon Clutch's secretary.'

'Myfannwy. Yes. She might give us Clutch's movements. And the porters, Trice and Ashwood, might be
able to give us Teape and Truegrave's if they were in
the building.'

'If you take the porters,' Theodora said, 'I'll have a
word with Teape.'

'Why?'

'He might know about the captioning of the photograph in Truegrave's book.'

Tom stretched his arms behind him and leaned forward. 'There's nothing more we can do tonight, is
there? I should go home.'

Theodora smiled at him. He looked very young with his concentrated absorption in a single task, like a choir boy.

Through the open window came the sound of a ship's siren, immensely melancholy. Theodora thought of the unclaimed corpse. Why did no one miss it, cry out for it, want to mourn it? It seemed a terrible omission. She realised it was taking on mythic proportions in her imagination. In her tired state and her discontent with the attitudes of the members of the dinner party, the corpse seemed to stand for all the things the Church wouldn't acknowledge, the inanity, the irrelevance of politics.

'You should go home,' she agreed. 'I'll walk you to the end of the Stowage in case the foxes get you.'

Companionably, equals, partners, no strife or dominance between them, free of the games-playing which obsessed their elders and joined in a common enterprise, albeit an odd and disquieting one, they made their way from the house. Theodora propped the damaged door to behind them as they stepped out into the cool night air. The smell of the river came up from beyond the wall. It refreshed and drew them. Tom steadied his bicycle with one hand and caressed the stone with the other. Water chafed the steps downstream. Theodora became aware of another sound, the creak and splash of oars. She could just see a shape bending rhythmically forward and back, pulling away from the bank, making good speed as the craft entered the current. In the bow of the boat, catching a gleam of light as it moved out into the channel, was a shopping trolley.

'I didn't know Maggie was an oarswoman,' Tom said.

'Not the time or place for shopping either,' Theodora agreed.

CHAPTER NINE

The Office

The water from the miniature watering can dropped accurately round the stem of the pelargonium, darkening the compost. Myfannwy Gwynether felt it doing the plant good. She was a nurturer by nature. She turned the plant round so the other side got the light. Fair dos, she always said. Next she produced a feather duster from the bottom drawer of the filing cabinet and ran it over her desk and windowsill. On her desk were framed photographs of the twins, one of her husband, Dennis, and a nice black and white of the cottage in Cwm Riath to which they would retire in three years' time when Dennis finished at the DHSS. The photographs were arranged on crocheted mats. Mrs Gwynether's hobby was macramé.

It was an orderly, it was a genteel environment, Mrs Gwynether felt. She sought the integrated life. At the office she liked to be reminded of her family; at home she enjoyed talking of her work for the Church. She made it sound as though the institution was in her debt, which, in a sense, it was, though it repaid her by allowing her to feel she was at the centre of things. Canon Clutch was a very important man who often had contact with people whose names appeared in newspapers and whose faces cropped up on the telly. 'We work very closely with every branch of Government,' Canon Clutch had told her. And indeed she had his diary to prove it. Lunch with permanent private secretaries at the Foreign Office, the occasional state banquet and livery company dinner were known of. Only yesterday he'd said, 'We have consultative rights with HM Government in a number of fields,' and he'd smiled his collusive smile. 'I make sure we hold them to it. These politicians need watching like hawks. If they're going to use the worldwide network of the Anglican communion, they'll have to pay for it.' Mrs Gwynether had not quite understood this one but over the years she'd got used to a certain degree of hyperbole in Canon Clutch's utterances. She attributed it, pleasant woman, to his getting carried away with an enthusiasm for his work.

It was a tiny office with something of the quality of an eyrie, a tower room where spells, or anyway something, was woven. There wasn't actually a cauldron in the corner but there might have been. If you stood in the small square in the middle of the room you could more or less reach everything else in it. The desk with two telephones, the two filing cabinets, the computer table and the hat stand were all under Mrs Gwynether's hand.

The first part of the morning ritual completed, Mrs Gwynether took her teacup and saucer (she felt mugs were common) to the electric kettle stationed on the smaller of the two filing cabinets. There she arranged the wherewithal for brewing the first of four teas of the day. While she waited she switched on the computer, first with foot and then with hand, and looked through the pile of envelopes Trace had left on her desk as Canon Clutch's share of the morning post. She had done the same thing every day for twelve years. She liked to feel the place coming alive around her bit by bit. It was like being present at creation; part was added to part until finally the whole place was connected together as a world, a harmonious whole, and she was in touch with it all. The computer system she'd taken to as though it had always lurked somewhere in her consciousness. 'Ami Pro plus Microsoft Three keeps you ahead of the game is what I always say,' she always said to the temps who rapidly succeeded each other in the general office. People had been surprised by how quickly she'd mastered the new technology, but really it wasn't so far removed from macramé when you came to think of it. You could play games on it. And she liked the different typefaces. You could get even boring memoranda looking lovely if you took the trouble. If people were occasionally disconcerted to find three different typefaces on a single side of A4, she was unaware of it; what were they there for if not to be used to cheer us all up? She was learning the graphics bit at the moment and had planned something really fancy for the documents due out around Christmas time.

She wasn't pleased to have the internal telephone ring before nine fifteen. Canon Clutch wasn't due in for another hour and those familiar with her working practices should have known she wasn't to be disturbed yet. However, 'I need your help, Myfannwy,' was a good beginning. She liked Tom Logg who, she surmised, might not last long given Canon Clutch's feelings about him. He was too keen on modern methods, was Tom. Computers were one thing, that was a matter of control and that was fine, someone had to control things. But you didn't want people stepping out of their proper places. Tom seemed to think things ought to work. He kept on wanting to review what was done and do it better, which meant different, which Mrs Gwynether didn't hold with. And she reckoned she had Canon Clutch on her side in that one. Change was not what he was for. So either Tom would learn or Tom would leave.

'If you want to pop down now, Tom, I can give you just a few minutes. I'm rushed off my feet at the moment.' She poured the boiling kettle into the cup with a steady right hand and held the phone in her left, reviewing the patience cards coming up on the computer screen with a practised eye.

Tom had given some thought to his tale. 'It's a time and motion study,' he told her.

Mrs Gwynether didn't bother to conceal her scepticism. 'Bit old hat, isn't it?'

This threw Tom. 'It's had a resurgence. The latest thing,' he assured her.

'Well, go on then. I'll have a go. And if you want to put that cup down, don't put it on the wood. It makes a nasty mark. There's a mat to your left.'

Tom, squeezed into the little cell and seated on a collapsible chair kept for visitors, brought out his organiser. 'The thing is, the arrangements for the Archimandrite weren't, would you say, smooth?'

Mrs Gwynether reserved her judgement until she was sure who was going to be blamed. That's what she had against reviewing things that were over and done with. Someone always got to be blamed – or that, anyhow, was how the clergy always interpreted it.

'And we do have a lot of public occasions. I mean important people, celebrities, photocalls, TV, national newspapers. We need to get it right.' It was Tom's motto.

Mrs Gwynether responded selectively. 'Celebrities, I wouldn't say. Not showbusiness and that lot. *Important* people, some of the highest in the land, yes.' She reverted to older categories.

'Right. So we need to get a set of systems in place.'

Mrs Gwynether sighed.

'Systems,' Tom pursued, 'which mean we all know how to handle every eventuality.' Tom did not say that even he was doubtful about how they would ever get in place systems which would dispose of the corpses of visiting dignitaries.

'What had you in mind, then?' Mrs Gwynether saw he would have to have his say.

'I think it would help if we knew who did what when. Then we can study the movement and see if there's duplication and time overlap. For example, if we start with Canon Clutch. When did he get in on Monday morning?'

'He wasn't too pleased, having his own routine put out. He had to be in quite a bit earlier than usual to get on top of the job.' Tom let this one go. 'He got in about a quarter to ten. Then,' Mrs Gwynether consulted the diary, a working version, not the gold-paged one on Canon Clutch's desk, 'he had the General Purposes at ten-thirty. Then he saw you about the arrangements for tea and the TV people. He went for lunch about twelve.'

'He didn't see Canon Truegrave or Canon Teape during the morning?'

'Not so far as I know. Canon Truegrave didn't get in till just after one. I heard him come down the corridor and look into the office for Canon Clutch but of course he'd gone for lunch by then.'

'What time did Canon Clutch get back?'

'Oh, he was back early. One-thirtyish. I know because I brought sarnies so as to be available if anything should crop up.'

'How about Canon Teape? I saw him taking a late lunch, round about two-thirty. Did he come up here after that?'

'I do keep a movement sheet for him but he's not always that up to date. Let's see what we can find.' Mrs Gwynether tapped her key and nodded her head up and down from board to screen. Tom saw the file list flash up and as quickly off again to reveal what he partially already knew. Lunch 1.30 to 2.30. Archbishop arrives 3.45. Tea 4 p.m. Signing 5 to 7 p.m. And then an individual item: Institute of Archivist Annual General Meeting at Dr Williams Library at 8.30 p.m. Heavy day for Teape.

'How about Truegrave?'

Mrs Gwynether rattled her keys again. 'He's very irregular. He doesn't always give me his movements. More in weeks or even months.' She pressed the key. Monday, 4 October. 'It doesn't say anything at all,' she said triumphantly.

'But he must have known he was due to meet the Archbishop, and the Archimandrite's a friend of his,' Tom objected.

'Yes, well, there you are.' Mrs Gwynether was philosophical. 'That's life for you, isn't it, a blank screen. I think Canon Truegrave feels that since *he* knows where he's going he doesn't *need* to put it down for anyone else.'

'But the whole point of a movements sheet is . . .' Tom could scarcely comprehend such attitudes. 'Where is Canon Truegrave now?'

The screen showed Wednesday, 6 October, 4.30 p.m. Azbarnahi exhibition Galaxy Gallery.

'Who types these things in?'

'I usually do. No. I tell a lie. I *always* do for Canon Clutch and Canon Teape. Canon Truegrave can type directly into this from his own terminal. Only, as I say, Canon Truegrave doesn't see the point. And sometimes Canon Teape jots it down for me and gives it me that way. Old habits die hard, don't they, Tom? We're not all computer literate yet, are we? Myself, I look forward to the day of the superhighway. Cyberspace is what we need.'

Tom, who had learnt Computer Studies since he was eleven (it was the one thing his school had done well), who had typed his notes at school and university as a matter of course, could only shake his head in agreement. Though what the Church of England would do with cyberspace he boggled to think.

'Let's come back to Monday. Canon Clutch. Where was he between one-thirty and two-thirty? Have you any idea?'

'He was in his room so far as I know.' Mrs Gwynether nodded her head in the direction of the Canon's state apartment next door.

'You'd have heard if he'd left it?' Tom knew the answer before she spoke. He'd made it his business to know this difficult and deceiving building.

'Well, not really, unless he'd actually come down this way. This is the main way, of course, but he could have gone by the small staircase, though it's not really meant for anything but the service staff. Not quite grand enough for the Canon, if you see what I mean. This door,' she nodded to her own cubbyhole's entrance, 'was open all during lunch. I like to get a bit of air in over the break. He didn't come past this way, that I am sure of, until he walked down with Canon Teape and Canon Truegrave to meet the Archbishop at about three.'

'Clutch and, I think, Teape were coming up the centre stair soon after two-thirty,' Tom said. 'We're about half an hour out.'

Mrs Gwynether looked thoughtful. 'The diary says,' she flipped over the pages, 'Archbishop arrival at three forty-five main entrance. And they did pass me to get there, as I said. But before that Canon Teape and Canon Truegrave passed me at about ten to three to go to Canon Clutch's office.'

'So they, Canon Clutch and Teape, must have gone the long way round the service staircase to get to the central staircase and be going up it and seen by me at just after two-thirty. Yes?'

'Yes, I suppose so.'

'Why should they do that?'

'How should I know?' Mrs Gwynether was getting flustered. 'I suppose it depends where they started from.'

'I know where Teape started from I saw him in the refectory.'

Mrs Gwynether had had enough. 'If this is time and motion study, I think it's going to use up a lot of my time. I think you'd better let me get on with some proper work for a change.'

'Right. Thanks, Mrs G.' Tom snapped back into his

professional mode. 'I've made a very careful note. You've been a great help. I'm sure it'll be of use next time we have important visitors. Though we don't want this sort of thing to happen too often, do we?'

To Theodora, minded to spend a couple of hours over lunch at Ecclesia Place library, Anona Trice's presence was just what she could do without. Also, she resented Anona coming without an invitation. Also, she noticed, she was frightened of Anona, of the extremity of her emotions. Theodora was not without experience. In the course of her diaconate she'd coped perfectly competently with many types of human failure, wickedness or sickness. If Anona should have a fit of hysteria or epilepsy, if she should tear her hair or find herself homeless, Theodora would know exactly what to do, what to say, who to ring or, more importantly, how to listen and wait. But this was not what Anona was going to do. The demure figure seated cross-legged on Theodora's newly sanded and polished floorboards was, somehow, more threatening, at a greater remove from the normal, explicable, predictable pattern. Anona was a wrecker, a nugget of unmanageable chaos waiting to explode in her living room.

Theodora had come back after the parish staff meeting to find Anona ensconced in her flat, thumbing through her copy of the *Tablet*. Theodora could see she'd have to get the front door lock mended, not just to keep her few possessions in but to keep visitors out. Theodora recognised she was failing here. She needed to reflect and work on demands which were beginning to emerge as incompatible. On the one hand she acknowledged the need for Christian hospitality. She knew many clergy who genuinely kept open house and if this was sometimes a toll on their families, it often paid off in terms of the trust and respect in which they were held in a parish. Geoffrey had started down that path before his marriage. She didn't think Oenone intended to encourage him. On the other hand she needed, she thirsted for privacy, calmness, place and time which she could order, control as she wished. 'The feminist ideal which sees power as a struggle for privacy,' she quoted to herself.

So now seeing Anona invading her space, calmly browsing her way through her paper, filled her with irritation. But then, she caught herself up, what did Anona, whose wishes might be similar to her own, have for herself?

'You see, Miss Braithwaite, Theo, if I may, Gilbert says there are correct and incorrect ways of living.'

Theodora nodded. Pretty safe that. Few would quarrel with that one.

'And games and dreams can help to grasp those ways.'

Less good, more dangerous, Theodora thought. What had Gilbert, what had little Mrs Trice in mind?

'Well, I have this dream, Theo, where I play a game. It's a sort of chess game, only for healing. A transformation game, Gilbert calls it. It's a therapy. He calls it the ludic element.'

Does he so? Theodora was cantankerous. Putting bits of oneself on to pieces and juggling them around to make new patterns, new selves; an American idea. She'd heard of it.

'It's safer, you see, Gilbert says.' Anona sounded as though she could do with some reassurance on this point.

Gilbert says, Gilbert says, Theodora muttered. What was Gilbert doing to the woman? Therapy was one thing, manipulation, control another. If Gilbert wanted to experiment with fashionable gewgaws like transformation games, he should try them with personalities less precariously balanced than she judged Anona to be.

'Only you've got to have the right pieces.'

'What are the right pieces?' It seemed the obvious question.

'They've got to be powerful. Things that mean something to you.'

'Such as?'

'It's surprising really how common these things are. Gilbert has some you can borrow. Though he says you've got to collect things for yourself as well, if it's going to work.'

Hell's teeth, thought Theodora. What diabolic little box of tricks did Gilbert keep in his top floor flat at St Sylvester's?

'Keys, rings, spoons, masks, anything really. Candles, cups,' Anona chanted on.

'And you shake a dice or play a card and move the

pieces according to a convention, a board, and then read the relationship between them?'

'That's right and you can see what's going to happen.' Anona caught herself up. 'No. That's wrong. Gilbert says you can't do that, you can only see what you are or might be.'

'Then it shows you what you already know.' Theodora tried to keep the exasperation out of her voice.

'It shows you things you didn't know. It frees you from . . .' Anona stopped. 'It frees you from yourself.'

'But yourself is exactly what you have to deal with. You can't get rid of it, only modify it a bit, push it in the right direction.'

'But I've been stuck for so long. I've waited so long. The game does seem to give me hope of a new start. And it can influence the world. It can draw things to you or back to you.'

'You can't get a new start from a game. Only by patient continuance in well-doing.'

'I thought you'd understand.' Anona's tone suggested it was Theodora's fault. Theodora was aware of how often she'd found herself in this position. People wanted a cure from their ills on their own terms without any moral or religious effort on their part. They wanted, in fact, magic. It was greedy, it was unrealistic. Gilbert shouldn't be fostering such a spirit.

'I understand all right. I just don't agree.' She wondered if she should add that Anona should be careful. It really wasn't possible to set limits to what patients would do with the toys provided by therapists. Fantasy wasn't therapeutic.

'Then you won't help me?'

'What sort of help had you in mind?'

'I need a new piece. So I can establish proper relations again.' Anona was near to tears.

'What sort of new piece?'

'I thought you'd be sure to know.'

CHAPTER TEN

The Exhibition

'I know what I'm supposed to do and I'm doing it, see?' Kevin Trace was talking to himself. He was rewriting a recent scene with Sergeant Ashwood. Only this time he, Kevin, was winning. It wasn't that Kevin hadn't met people in his life who told him what to do. His stepfather – correction, fathers – had often told him what to do with himself. Teachers, too, had told him to do things, though after a bit they had stopped on the grounds that it was hopeless. His probation officer, at his last meeting with that gentleman, had leaned, in friendly fashion, across the table and said, 'Kevin, old lad, let me give you a bit of advice before we part. Do to others what you would like them to do to you. See what I mean?'

Kevin had sort of seen. But there had to be a start somewhere. What he was looking for was someone doing to him what he *wanted* done to him. Then he could do a bit back. It was supposed to be the Church, wasn't it? Christians were supposed to be different, weren't they? The trouble with Christian brother Ashwood was, he didn't give you a chance. It was as if he liked giving orders more than anything else. He built himself up at your expense.

'We're all under orders, see?' Ashwood had told him. 'I got my orders here,' he tapped the clipboard. 'Them lot up there,' he nodded his head in the direction of the staircase, 'that lot've got their orders too.'

'Well, where does it all start then?' Kevin had asked. Who gives the first lot of orders, he meant.

'In Ecclesia Place they start with Canon Clutch,' Ashwood had answered.

'And who gives him them then?' This had stumped Ashwood.

'Nobody gives Canon Clutch orders. He's in charge, see? Senior Officer.'

Kevin had not seen. Why should some give orders and others not? Like he said, he knew what he was doing, he could see what was needed to keep the place running. He didn't need Ashwood or Canon Clutch telling him all the time. *He* didn't feel the need to start giving orders to anyone. All this lining up and drilling was just plain stupid, more for Ashwood's benefit than his, Kevin reckoned. Made them all feel safe. He'd considered jacking it in but there was money at the end of the week, and he couldn't face his mother if he didn't give this one a try.

He pushed the wheely bin faster to get up a bit of impulsion before reaching the ramp which led from the basement to the courtyard passage of Ecclesia Place. He wondered if he could link the bins together to cut down the number of journeys and make for a bit of interest in the cornering. He revved himself up for the final dash. The trolley, in the manner of trolleys, was insufficiently balanced for coping with its load. It lurched, locked and precipitated the bin on to the paving stones. Kevin said a number of things he'd heard his stepfathers say in their time.

'Hello,' said Tom. 'Having a bit of bother?'

Kevin looked at the spreading line of rubbish which was beginning to be blown about by the draught from the narrow passage.

'Just my flaming luck.'

'Not luck, knowledge. Technique.' Tom was didactic. He assumed everyone wanted to learn, Kevin as well as Canon Clutch. 'If you want to use that trolley to take that load at that angle, you'll need to reset the wheels at least another twenty centimetres out at the front.'

Kevin listened because Tom had started in to help him reassemble the rubbish. If Tom had just stood there, Kevin wouldn't have given ear.

'It looks past its boot,' Tom said, bundling newspapers and tea bags back into the bin as though it didn't matter who did what.

'Other one would be better. It's like what you said, wheels are fitted further out.'

'Why not use it?'

'It's broken. I hit it a bit of a clout Monday. I was in a hurry.'

Tom paused. 'Any particular reason?'

'They were all on edge because of that foreign bloke. Everything had to be, like, polished up. Ashwood kept on at me.'

'Did you get a look at the foreign chaps?' Tom was curious to know what Kevin might think of this new connection of the Church of England's.

'Yeh,' Kevin was smug. 'Got him all to meself, didn't I? He come before the main lot. I reckon Ashwood only got the second division. The runners-up.'

'What?' Tom was mystified.

'Like I said. The chief chap come early. Ten to oneish. Ashwood wasn't back from his little rest. This chap came in in a helluva hurry. I says to him, I says, "Sir, you've got to sign the book." Then Canon Truegrave trots up and takes him by the elbow and says, "That's all right, he's with me. Can you get us some coffee? The Archi whatever's had a long journey. He's a bit tired." So I scoots off and gets him some coffee.'

'Where did you take it to?' Tom was so close to Kevin he could see the youth's incipient moustache.

'I took it up to Canon Truegrave's office, but they weren't there. So I left it.'

'Then you came back here?'

'S'right. Just got in before the sergeant returned. He'd have said I shouldn't have left the desk. But needs must when the devil drives.' It was a phrase of his

144

nan's. Kevin thought it appropriate for the clerical context.

'How did you know it was the Archimandrite?'

'Got one of the cross things on his middle, silver with a big blue stone in it and a ring, big, foreign like.'

'But I did ask you before if you'd seen the Archimandrite and you said you hadn't.' Tom thought of all the time wasted.

'No you didn't.' Kevin was virtuous. 'You said had I seen anyone round about threeish. Well, I hadn't. I didn't see any of them again. Ashwood kept me at it clearing up the conference room right through the telly and that. He's a mean beggar.'

'You didn't happen to notice his boots, by any chance?'

'Nice pair. Funny colour. Brown.'

The tide was high as Theodora strode across Better-house Bridge. She felt the elation which comes from being suspended high over water. Scullers in skiffs looked stripped and athletic as they shot the piers of the bridge to emerge triumphant on the other side, as though they had performed some sort of conjuring trick. The floating pontoon with its fringe of small moored craft, rowing boats and canoes, which provided a quay for the river police launches, rose gently on the swell. In mid-channel, pleasure craft chugged and lurched as they changed places with each other. These would be the last trips of the year.

A Dutch motor barge pushed upstream to the last of

the commercial wharves beyond Betterhouse. The German flag flew from its stern. On the aft deck, behind the tiny wheelhouse, Theodora could make out two figures conversing. The height of the tide and hence the nearness of the boat to the bridge enabled her to see them quite clearly. One man, middle-aged and portly, wore a panama hat with an MCC ribbon and a fawn linen suit. The other, younger and slimmer, with thick black hair and sunglasses, wore blue overalls. On the deck between them a packing case vibrated to the throb of the engine. For a moment Theodora felt a pang of envy. How agreeable it would be to be going travelling on some commercial packet to see new places. Did one need a passport to go to Europe now? Or could she just step on board and bargain for a passage to Hamburg or Santander? Was that what the river was, an image of freedom, a natural highway to elsewhere? Was that why it drew people, to stare over the parapets of bridges, to stand on tiptoe to peer over flood barriers, to hang about quays and wharves? Was that why she'd chosen to live beside the river? She caught herself up. She'd just told Anona Trice not to fantasise. She had work to do here. Quite apart from the parish and its worthwhile tasks, something was going on at Ecclesia Place which had led to a man's, perhaps a priest's, death. Who had killed the man in Tom's photograph and why? And who was he?

Ashwood, at the reception desk of Ecclesia Place, greeted her by name. He'd obviously added her to his list of regulars.

'Is Mr Logg in, Sergeant?'

'Left for lunch at,' he consulted his book, 'twelve thirty. Should be back any time now. Very punctual man, Mr Logg. He left a message in case you called.'

It was Theodora's theory that Ashwood couldn't bend from the waist. He hinged from the top of his legs and reached under the counter and produced an envelope.

'And is Canon Teape in?'

'Came in ten a.m. No note of him having left. If he's not in the library, you could try the refectory. He lunches late, the archivist.'

Tom's note read, 'Kevin holds the clue. Gone to exhibition. Will call *c.* eight this evening. OK?'

Theodora headed for the library, making her way down to the foundations of the building. Teape was nowhere to be found. The library had the air of indifference to people which characterises the best libraries. It existed for itself alone. In fact there were a couple of what Theodora classified as postgraduate theologians closeted in the corner of one of the bays but they seemed swallowed up in the silence. The big catalogue was in the centre of the room. It had not progressed beyond a set of handwritten cards some with the ink turning green with age – slotted onto metal rods.

Theodora checked the reference number of Ellis Bernhardt Truegrave's copy of *The Cold War Frontiers and the Church*. The library did not use the Dewey system but some arcane symbolism of its own. Theodora, however, was an old hand at cracking the systems of theological libraries. She mounted the neat spiral staircase to the upper catwalk and put her hand on the volume. The book opened at the photograph labelled 'Georgios XII, Archimandrite of All Azbarnah 1974-'. There, as Tom had said, was the studio black and white of a strong-featured man in his fifties, bareheaded, set against a white wall with a black Orthodox cross on it. Her eye travelled down the heavy figure and, yes, there it was, the pectoral cross which could easily have been the one so lately in her possession.

She scrutinised it for some minutes. There was no attribution to a photographer. She flicked to the contents page, then to the illustrations. Maps from the *Times Atlas*, photographs, courtesy of Canon E. B. Truegrave. So he'd taken it himself. Had he labelled it correctly? Where had the mistake, if it was a mistake, come? Theodora looked at the pendulum clock on the wall above the archivist's desk. It was two-thirty. She really couldn't linger here. There was work to be done in the parish. As she turned to descend, there was a shuffling sound at the far end of the room and Canon Teape appeared stage left behind his desk.

Theodora gathered up the volume and made her way down the stairs and round the catalogue. Teape gave a theatrical start.

'Miss Braithwaite, how very nice. Have you everything you want? There is some of Newcome's early correspondence catalogued, rather confusingly perhaps, under Revival, Catholic.'

Theodora wasn't interested in the eccentricities of the Ecclesia Place archive catalogue. She looked down at Teape's toad-like figure. She noticed he was actually younger than she had thought on first meeting. His thin hair, watery eyes and recessive manner had made him seem older than his probable middle forties. That meant, perhaps, that he might be more clued up than an older cleric. For a moment she played with the idea of showing him the photograph and inviting his comment. Would he recognise that the photograph of Georgios XII was not the man whom he had met with Archbishop Papworth a couple of days ago? But something restrained her.

'I was thinking of going to the Azbarnahi exhibition.'

'Ah, at the Galaxy Gallery. I haven't got round to it myself yet but it's supposed to be very good. I'm afraid we haven't been sent the catalogue.'

'Background reading,' Theodora explained.

'Very necessary, otherwise objects lose their significance. One puts them in the wrong context or no context at all. We tend to think our own categories are the only ones and then miss the point. We used to call it education.'

'Quite.' Theodora was terse. Why did she feel so irritated with the Ecclesia Place set-up? It had done her no harm. On the other hand it didn't seem to do anyone any good either.

Canon Teape glanced at the volume in Theodora's hand. 'I see you have Bernhardt's little volume. Quite a good introduction to something of a *terra incognita*.

The article by Cyril Leyland on the art and architecture is particularly well researched.'

Theodora took the plunge. 'I was wondering about the illustrations. The one of the Archimandrite attributed to Canon Truegrave. That would have been taken by himself, would it?'

'Oh, yes. Bernhardt is a very competent photographer. He did a beautiful job on my own small collection.'

'You collect?'

'In a modest way, ecclesiastical silver.'

'Not incunabula?'

'One sees so many books.' Canon Teape was deprecating.

'And the Ecclesia Place Press,' Theodora was dogged. 'I haven't come across it before. Are they . . .' She wanted to say capable of carrying out proof-reading which would get the photographs rightly labelled. 'Look,' she said, and slid the volume under Teape's nose. 'I wondered if there was a mistake.'

Teape studied the photograph for a minute or two. 'Mistake?' he said wonderingly. 'How?'

'The man in the photograph doesn't look much like the man I saw on *News at Ten* the other night.'

'Really? I suppose the TV lighting is rather different. A treacherous medium.'

Theodora was stumped. 'Is this really the same man you sat across the table from to negotiate the concordat on Monday?'

'Oh yes,' said Teape. 'No doubt at all.'

*

Tom pushed at the door marked pull, reconsidered his position and pulled. The young woman inside the door of the Galaxy Gallery shone like an icon. She had gold hair and was dressed in a gold and black dress with long black sleeves. Gold slippers peeped from under her table, on which was heaped a pile of catalogues.

She ran her eye up and down Tom from his brossed hair via the nylon shirt and grey flannel suit to a Reading University cycling club tie. She took in his crepe-soled French shoes. These had done him good service on his final year's studies exchange at Lyons' Institut de Finances Commerciales. He wasn't too easy to read, he knew.

'We're just closing.' She'd made her decision. Her accent could have been Benenden via Sloane Square.

Tom smiled collusively and bent towards her. 'I'm doing some research for Canon Truograve of Ecclesia Place.'

The girl hesitated. 'I don't think he's left yet. You might just catch him in salle number two.'

The form of the gallery, its systems and mechanisms, were unfamiliar to Tom and therefore meat and drink. 'Who's sponsoring the exhibition, I mean financially?'

The assistant was surprised. 'You are. I mean, Ecclesia Place is.'

Tom was thrown. 'Are you sure?'

The girl's gold eyebrows indicated she thought he was joking tastelessly. She handed him a catalogue and dismissed him.

Tom stepped through the door marked 'Salle One'

and stopped. The room was dark and for a moment he had to adjust his eyes. There was a smell of incense and, only just discernible above the velvety silence, the sound of slow bass chanting. Down the middle of the room was a line of modern glass cases like a jeweller's, each illuminated from its base and shining like baubles anchored on a dark sea. In each had been placed a collection of homogeneous objects, icons, ciboriums, plates, pyxes, office books in elaborate silver bindings. The effect was of an unsung and uncelebrated but illustrated Mass. Overall, suspended from the ceiling in the middle of the room, was a cross, two metres by two, in silver with a pattern of blue opaque stones the size of a man's hand worked into the design. The light from the showcases below played on it and it swung in the breeze of the ventilation system like a mobile.

The elaborate creation of this ambience without a context in life disturbed Tom. What sort of response did the organisers want? What was the point of artificially constructing a church without the essential purpose of a church, for worship. Was Ecclesia Place really sponsoring this?

More to the point, where was Truegrave? Tom wanted to ask that gentleman about one or two things. Like, what did you do with the Archimandrite between collecting him too early for the concordat meeting, his becoming a corpse and his disappearing from the carpet I rolled him in at about two-thirty, before you met a man who is different from someone you photographed and labelled Archimandrite Georgios XII in your book *The Cold War Frontiers and the Church*? Difficult, Tom thought, to put it more succinctly than that.

Salle number one ended in double doors covered by long purple curtains. The shock of light in salle number two made Tom blink. This room was bright with October evening sunlight reinforced by powerful fluorescent ceiling light. The cases here were of scale models of power plants, factories and office blocks. Round the walls were blow-ups of mining complexes and hydro-electric dams; the Vorasi factory and the Zakon dam – doing, doubtless, terrible things to the tributary of the Danube. Closer inspection showed them to be photographs taken at different and ingenious angles of the same dam and the same factory. Tom bent to look more closely at the enlargement of the machinery and products. So the Ecclesia Place Press weren't the only ones who could get the labelling of photographs wrong. The room, however, was empty.

'The exhibition will close in ten minutes,' said the Benenden voice from the grille in the wall. Then, lest there should be any monoglot Azbarnahi speakers, '*Kurkali sen verhoi ahlonzok dur instelin.*' The speaker, clearly not a native, stumbled over the vowels as though they were tank stops. Perhaps Azbarnahi was not taught at Benenden.

Tom dived back the way he'd come. Adjusting his eyes to the jeweller's room, he began to move towards the door by which he'd entered. Before he reached it, his ear was caught by the rustle of a curtain covering a door he'd not previously noticed halfway down the long side of the room. Curious, Tom swerved briskly towards it. The back stairs fire exit of the Galaxy Gallery opened before him. Below he could hear the sound of feet on metal treads. He leaned over and peered into the dimly lit lobby at the bottom. There was a sound of a bar being pushed on a door and, in the light which for a moment the open door admitted, Tom could make out the figure of a man in a black cassock. The man's face turned, momentarily, towards him. It was his second view of the Archimandrite Georgios XII, the one who had signed the concordat.

CHAPTER ELEVEN

The Agenda

'The agenda for the Diet, I need hardly tell you, should come before any other priority.' Canon Clutch never felt he need not repeat himself or shy away from what was perfectly understood by everyone. He smiled at his canon colleagues, almost winked at Myfannwy but by the time his eye reached Tom the smile had worn itself out.

The pre-meeting to the agenda meeting of the Diet was held in Clutch's room. It was as impressive as a cabinet minister's. Tom read the symbols to himself. There had been some interesting work done recently on the symbolism of workplace environments. But a lot of it was American and focused on factors like 'the placing of the mineral water machine in open working areas'. Perhaps he could offer something more sophisticated for *Modern Manager*'s Easter issue.

The cliff of mahogany desk reared up like a rampart to indicate straightforward power of the *ad baculum* variety. A cache of Kalashnikovs in a corner could hardly have been more blatant. Canon Clutch seated himself behind the desk but provided no other accommodation except chairs for his colleagues. They were expected to scribble uncomfortably on their laps and consult papers spread out on the floor.

An oil painting of the last but one Archbishop of Canterbury presided over all from behind Clutch's chair. It was considered tactful to wait until vacating office before sitting for a portrait. To forge too swiftly into the future would be imprudent. So the symbolism, no less potent, was always, as it were, one in arrears. The last but one occupant smiled self-deprecatingly at his lawn sleeves. His college's arms rested on his left ear. He'd been a scholar by inclination and had not wanted to be Archbishop. His retirement day had been a happy one. The gilt frame was topped with the arms of the see in gilded plaster. It gave the particular mould and form of power, ecclesiastical not just governmental.

Canon Clutch thumbed through the three-inch thick set of papers. Tom looked at his own contribution with pride: 'Proposed Agenda of Lay Diet Draft One'. It was beautifully produced. It had, as his first effort in the area, cost him much in time and research. The last five years which he'd scrutinised for models seemed to him to be the work of blundering amateurs in both layout and content. Whoever had done them previously had clearly not been up to date with Frachstein and Maddison's research on 'Business Paper Layout' in *Format and Focus*, Thodorakis and Vendor, Princeton UP 1993.

The way the agenda was put together needed looking at in Tom's view. As a system it lacked transparency. It had been impossible to detect who could put what items on. He shouldn't really have had to ask a typist how the agenda of the chief instrument of the government of the Church of England was produced, but Canon Clutch had brushed aside his questions as though they were impertinent. Myfannwy's account had been serviceable if impressionistic. 'Canon Clutch sees the chairmen of each of the three houses about a couple of months before the meeting. He doesn't usually go through the items with anyone for the laity or clergy. But he always goes through the bishops' stuff with the Archbishop of Canterbury, who chairs, and with the heads of section here, Canon Truegrave for Overseas Mission, Canon Teape for Theological Development; Canon Clutch himself does Home Affairs. The financial stuff comes in, usually at the last minute, by a different route, which to be honest I've never quite understood,' Myfannwy admitted. 'There's always a lot of paper from finance and a couple of accountants from down the road come and attend on the day in case there are any questions, which there usually aren't because it's all so complicated on the finance side of things. We all trust Canon Clutch because he's been doing it for so long.' Lots of work to do there, Tom thought with pleasure. Lots and lots of reforms obviously needed.

Tom uncrossed his legs and placed his organiser on his lap. He was alert and eager. He felt himself in the service of a great institution dedicated to the improvement of the human condition.

'We don't need to bother with the laity stuff,' said Canon Clutch. 'The important one is the House of Bishops.' He began to thumb through the pile of papers.

'We might think about colour coding for the future,' Tom offered helpfully.

Clutch ignored him. 'Myfannwy?'

Mrs Gwynether poked the file. 'There you are, Canon, about half an inch from the bottom.' She had the restrained patience of a secretary doing overtime for which there was no need and for which no one would thank her, let alone pay her. It was 6.15 p.m.

'Half an inch from the bottom,' Clutch amplified for those who could not hear. There was much shuffling of papers and looking over shoulders.

Tom, who had learned to read the signs even if he was not prepared to allow them to influence his own professional conduct, realised that Canon Clutch was nervous and therefore likely to erupt into anger. His cheek was hectic and the pulse in his right temple was throbbing. Not in good physical shape, Tom surmised. He wondered if he could interest him in cycling, from which so many benefits for health and environment were to be derived.

'Where's the laity material?' The inquiry came from Canon Truegrave.

'We're, er, not going to, er . . .' Canon Teape explained.

'What?' Truegrave adjusted his hearing aid.

'House of Bishops,' Clutch barked.

Mrs Gwynether extended an indicating finger. Tom gazed hard at Truegrave with whom he intended to have a word after the meeting. Right now Truegrave looked as though he was receiving messages from another planet. He had spread his fingers on his knees and was drumming them as though in time to unheard music, hissing the while through his teeth.

'The difficult item will be the concordat, won't it?' Canon Teape looked up. 'That is, isn't it, correct me if I'm wrong, Kenneth, the one you have in mind?'

'There is absolutely no reason at all to suppose that there'll be any opposition. I gave Papworth dinner at my club after the signing. He gave me his word.'

'Of course there'll be *opposition*,' said Truegrave as though making an original contribution.

'Why?' asked Tom.

Canon Teape and Canon Truegrave swung round on him.

'Because it means the Church spending money.' Teape sounded as though the point was so obvious it did not need saying.

'Because bishops are politically naive. They fail to recognise the immense political advantages of things like this.' Clutch did not apparently notice that this opinion contradicted his previous insistence that there would be no opposition.

'Because bishops don't know anything about anything if it's more than twenty miles from home,' Truegrave snapped. 'Unless of course it's in Africa or South America and they're mostly wrong there. About Europe they know nothing.'

'Have you considered where on the agenda you might put the Azbarnah item?' Tom pursued.

'It'll have to go first because the Archbishop will have to introduce it and the Archbishop could hardly come on at the end.' Teape was kindly instructive to Tom.

'Have you sounded out the possible voting patterns?' Tom was just interested in the mechanisms.

There was silence.

'I've told you, I dined with the Archbishop.' It clearly didn't occur to Clutch that there were other steps available.

'I'll tell you what we could do.' Teape crouched over his lily leaf and meditated a spring. 'We could get the Archimandrite to address the House of Bishops, speak for the cause, as it were.'

'Impossible,' said Truegrave, temporarily abandoning his deafness. 'He flew out yesterday evening.'

'But,' said Tom, 'I just . . .' then he stopped. The group looked at him.

'If you've nothing helpful to contribute, perhaps you could hold your tongue.' Clutch could have been addressing a child in a different century. Teape cleared his throat uneasily. Truegrave made deprecating hissing noises through his teeth. Myfannwy sucked her shorthand pencil. Only Tom gazed steadily at the overwrought canon and wondered what would make him crack up entirely, for clearly he was not rational.

'We could fly him back for the meeting,' Tom said to show there were no hard feelings. 'The Diet's four weeks off.'

'He goes into retreat for the whole of November,' Truegrave said.

'I don't know how you come to be so very familiar with the Archimandrite's diary,' Teape said in admiration.

'I think I may be his oldest friend,' said Truegrave with emotion. 'Anyway, he can only leave the country for very short periods of time. The whole situation is on a knife edge there. He has many enemies.' His tone was grave and concerned.

'And not just in Azbarnah,' Tom said.

'What do you mean by that?' Clutch was apoplectic. Tom had judged it right. It had got to Clutch. The man was sweating inside his lovely suiting. 'Since you have nothing useful to contribute you can leave us.'

'Yes, of course,' Tom said. 'I quite understand.' He might have been soothing a frightened horse. 'Just let me know what you decide and then we can think about the implementation bit.'

'I think cracks are beginning to appear,' Tom said into the telephone. 'Can you come over about eight?'

'Well,' Theodora was reluctant. 'We've got an evening Eucharist for the local church school staff and governors. It's something of a new venture and I really must be there.'

'Nineish?'

'Fatted Calf, nine-thirty, and I may be late.'

'Not the Calf. A bit too near. Do you know the all-night van, McClusky's, upstream under the arch of Betterhouse Bridge? Very good on bacon rolls. Maggie uses it. Yes? Well, there then. Are you free the rest of the night?'

Theodora groaned. 'Yes, yes. I had not intended to spend it in fasting and watchfulness.'

'Goody, goody.' Tom sounded so pleased it was impossible to deny him.

She put together the manuscript sheets of *Thomas Henry Newcome, A Life*, and placed them on the windowsill. She looked with regret at the tea chest which had served her so well over the last few weeks. Wednesday today. By the weekend she'd have unpacked the books from the last tea chest and would be faced with the tremendous moral dilemma of whether or not to buy a table. It would be convenient, she had to admit. But it was a possession which was not strictly necessary. And if a table, then chairs; a tight entailment. Just so does one thing lead to another. 'It's a slippery slope,' she said aloud.

For refreshment she stared out towards the river and gauged the time by the state of the tide. It should be about seven. The light had almost gone now and when the sun went down, autumn could be felt. St Sylvester's chime confirmed the hour. She loved the chime, loved the rhythm of the tide. Why could we not live rhythmically within the day, month and year, instead of gashing it all up with haste and anxiety. I'd like to do the same thing at the same time every day, she thought. And her mind went to the retreats she had made with religious orders. Then by a reasonable connection she thought about Anona Trice and Gilbert Racy. Why was she worried about Anona? Anona was Gilbert's responsibility. She'd known Gilbert ever since she came to the parish three years ago. She didn't doubt his integrity as a priest. She knew him to lead the appropriate disciplined life of prayer and abstinence which the Catholic tradition commends. She'd seen enough of his work with the mentally sick, those betrayed or bereaved, who had come to the end of some personal tether, to know that he would take exhaustive pains to aid their healing. He was qualified in psychology and had at least a partial training in medicine behind him. What made her feel he was treating Anona differently from other patients? Suddenly it occurred to her who might know.

She dialled the number and got the beginning of the answerphone message before it was switched off and the well-known voice answered.

'Oenone, Theodora Braithwaite here. Is Geoffrey about?'

'No, he's due back any minute. He's got a special Eucharist. I think he said it's for St Sylvester's primary school staff and governors. He wants it to be a success.'

'Yes,' said Theodora, carefully keeping impatience out of her tone.

'He's worked terribly hard at his sermon.'

'Has he really?' Theodora was tart. 'That's rather odd since I'm supposed to be preaching and I finished writing it last Saturday evening.'

'Oh.'

'*He's celebrating*.' Theodora stressed both words.

'Ah. I haven't quite got the jargon yet.' Oenone was dignified.

Theodora relented. 'I expect it's the sermon for the Rotary evensong on Friday he's preparing. That's new as well. Evensong's a bit of a departure for St Sylvester's.'

'I expect you're right.' Oenone, too, was willing to be forgiving. They were, after all, essentially from the same sort of stable. Theodora had worked at Oenone's smart school. There was nothing to deprecate, much less despise. Oenone had real virtues and talents. It was just odd that, with little beyond social convention to sustain her own religious life, she'd chosen to marry Geoffrey, as proper a priest as Theodora was a deacon. For Oenone it must be like learning a new language, supporting Geoffrey through his strange tergiversations.

'I wonder if you could do me a favour?' Theodora hedged against rejection.

'If I can.' Oenone's tone was level if not enthusiastic.

'It's Anona Trice. Do you happen to know who her husband is?'

'Oh, yes.' Oenone perked up. Here was a level playing field. 'I got it out of Geoffrey after the dinner party.'

'Ah,' said Theodora when she'd heard Oenone to the end. 'That's really very helpful. Yes, quite a new light.'

'*I* thought so too. By the way, I wondered if you could help. I'm trying to get rid of that table and the set of chairs which go with it from the kitchen. You may remember it. It's frightfully heavy and pig ugly. I'd like to pass it down the line so we can refit with something a bit more flexible.'

Theodora drew breath. The moment of choice had come. 'I think I know a home for it.'

Tom spread out the catalogue from his Azharnah exhibition on the rickety picnic table from which the middle plank was missing. Around their feet was a litter of paper cups and Coke cans. McClusky's at ten at night wasn't crowded. Overnight lorry drivers in nylon overalls and a couple of teenage girls in leathers was the sum of the clientele. Theodora, arriving in a rush, thought she saw Maggie at the periphery of the arc light generated by the van but when she looked again she saw nothing. Steam hissed from the van itself and the smell of delicious fried onions. Every now and again the hooter of a tug sounded from the other side of the flood wall. After the warm day there was a smudge of mist on the water.

Tom applied ketchup to his bacon roll. 'It's a good place, yes?'

'Fine.' Theodora fought with the sugar dispenser which was of the kind to discourage clients from over-indulging. 'So what do you reckon you've found out?'

Tom mopped his lips on a paper napkin and reached for his extra large coffee. He unscrewed the top of the sugar bottle and poured to his heart's content. Theodora watched in admiration. He was resourceful and would go far.

'What would you say Ecclesia Place is about?' he began.

'Power, obviously,' Theodora answered.

'What sort?'

'Political. Not, certainly, moral or religious. It sees itself very much as an arm of the Government, in-volved with it in law and finance, property, social policy, education. All those bishops in the Lords.' She sighed. 'However, what's that to do with Azbarnah?'

'That too is about politics and power and probably money as well.'

'No sex?' Theodora was dry.

'I haven't found any yet.' Tom took her seriously.

'And the clue is in the catalogue to the exhibition which you went to?' Theodora indicated the black and gold pages flapping in the breeze.

'There and elsewhere.' He flipped open the page which was already turned down and pushed it across.

Theodora began to read from the introduction. '"Azbarnah's rich artistic heritage rests almost entirely in the hands of a number of old landed families, the members of which supply the leaders of the Orthodox Church. Items in Salle One are on loan from the present Archimandrite of Azbarnah, Georgios XII, from whose personal collection they . . ." Personal collection?' Theodora pulled up. 'Hang on a minute. How can a priest have a personal collection? Surely they belong to the Church.'

'Press on.'

'"The Galaxy Gallery gratefully acknowledges the help of HM Foreign Office and the British Council in sponsoring this exhibition." So? That looks fairly innocuous.'

'The Galaxy Gallery staff think Ecclesia Place is financing it.'

'I don't see what you're getting at.'

'I saw the Archimandrite there. The TV one.'

'Where?'

'At the exhibition.'

'I'd gained the impression he'd flown out.'

'I'd gained that impression too. In fact, Truegrave explicitly said so at the pre-meeting, the meeting we've just had to set the agenda for the Diet next month. There are tensions there. I got the feeling at times that Teape anyway and perhaps Truegrave were playing with Clutch. Clutch is dead scared that the Diet won't ratify the concordat.'

'Why is it so important?'

'Right. Of course it could just be face. These three have put their combined weight behind it and don't

167

want it overturned. But the more interesting question is, why have they put their weight behind it in the first place?'

Theodora drew a pattern in spilled coffee on the table. 'Archie Douglas's remarks about a country of which we know little.'

'Quite. Why pick Azbarnah as a theatre for ecumenical ventures? You'd have thought there might be more respectable, less louche ones.'

'Ah,' said Theodora catching his drift, 'you mean HM Government might have an interest.'

'It is odd that the Church of England should just happen to be thinking about somewhere as unsavoury as Azbarnah at the same time as HM Government is sponsoring a trade mission there.'

'Are they?'

'I checked with an old mate of mine at the British Council.' Tom was smug. He liked his network to pay off. 'And from the Government's point of view, if you wanted to get a foothold in Azbarnah, a country with which we haven't had a diplomatic relation for forty years, wouldn't it be sensible to use an already existing network?'

'You mean Truegrave's Eastern European one?'

'He's got a staff of four people,' Tom said professionally. 'Three men and one woman. I had a look at the establishment list. It's a big set-up by Ecclesia Place standards. They've all got names like Lutolowski Robinson. By which I infer that they're native speakers. It's not an easy language, I believe. They're never in and I've not met one of them in nearly three months in post.'

'What would the Government be after that the Church could deliver?'

Tom tapped the exhibition catalogue. 'Part two of the exhibition shows that.' He turned the pages over and indicated the double-spread photograph.

Theodora gazed at the photograph of a processing plant. 'What is it for?'

'Irradium.'

'For aircraft?'

'Very necessary. Nearer to us and, given the rate of exchange of the szamki, cheaper than any other source. Would help us a lot and put us one up on France or Germany if we got a toe in first.'

'And who owns this thing?'

'The Turannidi, the family of the Archimandrite. They're hereditary landowners of most of the northern province.'

'How does that help you with your corpse?'

'Well, this is my final bit of evidence.' Tom smiled from ear to ear and flipped over the pages.

Theodora looked at the portrait of the Archimandrite Georgios XII in black and white. It showed the same features as the one in Bernhardt Truegrave's book. It was not the face she had seen on the TV on Monday night.

'So one thing is certain. The chap who appeared at the signing meeting and on TV isn't the Archimandrite. Our chap is younger and the true one is older for a start.'

'I thought there was something odd about him when I saw him with Papworth,' Theodora agreed. 'He shouldn't have crossed his legs.'

'What?'

'When he was interviewed with Papworth, the false Archimandrite crossed his legs. Orthodox clergy wearing cassocks don't do that. It's regarded as indecorous, even insulting.'

'That so?' Tom liked esoteric knowledge.

'And you think your corpse was the true Archimandrite?'

'He fits both pictures nicely.'

'So what was he doing outside the conference hall?'

'Waiting for the conference to begin.' Tom was complacent.

'But he was dead.' Theodora was irritated. 'And the reception party would have gone down to welcome him. He couldn't just have slipped in without anyone knowing. Ashwood would have noticed.'

'Just so. They did go down to welcome him, or at least Truegrave did.' Tom filled Theodora in on Kevin's intelligence. 'Myfannwy's account fits that and so does my seeing them, Clutch and Teape that is, drift up the staircase at around two forty-five. Say it worked something like this. Truegrave collects the true Archimandrite from Kevin in reception about ten to one. Perhaps Truegrave wanted a little talk about political matters before the main party arrived. Then Truegrave walks him down to the conference room and the chap pegs out.'

Theodora was intrigued. 'And while Truegrave went to get his colleagues, you came along and wrapped him in a carpet. Then what happened?'

'Nasty moment for Truegrave *et al*. Instigated a search and luckily stumbled over him just where you'd expect to find him, among the builders' rubble, in the room next to the conference hall.'

'What about boots?' Theodora was firm.

'I rather wonder if he wasn't using his hollow heels to carry one or two little items of value out of the country.'

Theodora sighed. 'Canon Teape collects ecclesiastical silver.'

'That so? Not a poor man's hobby.'

'So Gilbert said. In fact, it would make sense if the conversation I overheard Gilbert having on the phone the other morning was with Teape. That would explain why he had boots made for him with hollow heels.'

'Always useful. I shall follow the custom myself when I can afford to have my boots made.' Tom was clearly cruising towards home. 'On the other hand it does look as though they're all three in on this matter. Teape for his silver, Truegrave for his Eastern Europe empire and Clutch . . .'

'Clutch for the politics. HM Government and all that,' Theodora completed the picture. 'Did you know that Truegrave was married to Anona Trice?' she asked, seemingly at a tangent.

'That so? How did you find out?'

'Oenone got it from Geoffrey. I wondered, because at

their dinner party last night Gilbert made a thing of not wanting it revealed. Client confidentiality and all that.'

'What does she look like?'

'Big head, small body, cap of red-gold short hair.'

'I think I've seen her in the Place library,' Tom said.

'Doing what?'

'Don't know but she was up the catwalk in the area where her husband's book is. Do you think she's mixed up in this?'

Theodora shook her head. 'She's very keen to draw her husband back to her. She plays a game, half chess, half magic, in order to bring it about. I suppose she wasn't here on Monday when they were shifting the body about?'

'She's not in Ashwood's book, though that doesn't mean much.'

'I suppose it's not really very likely. However, what *did* they do with the body when they found it?'

'It might still have been in the basement area when we looked for it on Monday night, in a wheely bin, minus a boot.'

'And where is it now?' Theodora wanted to keep Tom down to earth.

'In the freezer?'

Theodora shuddered. 'Why?'

'They can't pass the false Archimandrite off as the true one in Azbarnah because he's known there. So they'll have to produce a body and acknowledge the death, but try and make out he died after he'd done the concordat signing. Then they'll need to put in someone as Archimandrite who will keep to the terms of the concordat. Truegrave *will* be busy.'

'And where does the false Archimandrite come from?'

'Well, if you remember, he was late. Kept Canon Clutch's cucumber sandwiches cooling. My bet is that Truegrave was told to find a substitute.'

'One of his young men stacked in the flat under the flight path for Terminal Two at Heathrow,' Theodora contributed.

'Eh?'

'He entertains a lot of young men from Azbarnah from the University of Vorasi. But why not just announce that the true Archimandrite had had a heart attack and abandon the party?'

'Depends what was hanging on the signing, HM Government and all that. We all have our reasons for not admitting to death,' Tom said soberly. 'I wasn't going to jeopardise my career. Canon Clutch *et al* weren't going to put the Church of England's – well, Ecclesia Place's – credibility at risk with the Foreign Office. If they thought that the Archimandrite's death would put an end to the concordat signing, perhaps indeed to the concordat itself, especially if the whole thing depended heavily on Truegrave's special relationship with the family of the Archimandrite, they might be moved to extreme measures.'

'It's all speculative,' Theodora said. 'On the other hand you have a body, no doubt about that. You also have a false Archimandrite and there has to be some explanation for that. If you're right about the Foreign Office-Ecclesia Place link, it could just be. Frankly,' she added, 'I'd believe anything of the FO. I had a cousin there who would stoop to anything.'

'Cousin?'

'He was my father's elder brother's wife's youngest nephew.'

'Do you know him well enough to tap into?' Tom was urgent. 'I mean we really do need some confirmation of the FO-Ecclesia Place link re Azbarnah.'

Theodora considered how well she knew Julian Morely-Trump. 'I could try. I haven't seen him since I was fourteen. Meanwhile . . .'

'Meanwhile I think we should have a go at internal evidence.'

Theodora put the rest of the cold coffee inside her. Together they made their way down back alleys and side passages, meeting and parting from the river as history dictated, in the direction of the more respectable quarter of Ecclesia Place.

CHAPTER TWELVE

The Computer

'How about keys?'

'Did a deal with young Kevin. He isn't paid until Friday.'

Theodora wasn't sure she approved. But it made it easier to move around Ecclesia Place in the dark than the last time they'd come. Tom headed off from the entrance hall up the main staircase, jangling his prizes.

'The trouble is that there's no communication between the different branches of the Place's administration. Each department has its own hardware and software. I've counted seven makes of hardware and there's probably double that of software packages. Every time you want to run a disk on a machine other than your own you've got a major conversion job on hand.'

Theodora listened with half an ear. The parish had
run to an Amstrad. It looked a bit old-fashioned, made
a noise when printing but was otherwise un-
temperamental. She knew no one who would want to
borrow it.

'They still write memos to each other, if they communicate at all.' Tom was scornful. 'They could put
the day's notices straight on to the computer link and
then of course they could connect it to phones, including mobiles. Save an enormous amount of secretarial
time.'

'Why don't they then?' They rounded a corridor and
plunged back into the grid system which Theodora
always found so confusing.

'I've given it some thought.' Tom was judicious. 'The
Church doesn't actually value knowledge which it
hasn't itself discovered. So management and communications skills, social and psychological sciences,
even finance and law are all seen as either irrelevant
or a threat. Of course it makes life easier in a way,
instead of listening and learning you can just ponti-
ficate. It's a very eccentric culture.'

Theodora, who knew far more than Tom about the
impermeable, ignorant smugness of senior clergy,
thought he'd been rather bright to come to this conclusion so quickly. She, after all, had the advantage of
inheritance.

'Do you know,' Tom went on, fumbling for keys to
the door marked 'Eastern European Affairs – Canon
E. B. Truegrave', 'I've sat in a room full of lawyers,

some of whom we've been paying, and listened to *Clutch* tell *them* what the law is. No wonder they smile at us.' The door swung open and Tom switched on the light.

It was a scene of chaos. Books, papers, computer disks and glasses of lemon tea lay over the floor. A photograph in a silver frame of a man in nineteenth-century military uniform with whiskers and a sword had had its glass broken. On the wall a Russian two-barred cross hung but hung crooked. A couple of icons on either side had been displaced and were similarly awry.

They both surveyed the scene in silence.

'Someone's done it over,' Tom said finally.

'Who, and looking for what?' Theodora felt the assault on possessions as though they had been her own. She sensed hatred and unreason behind the mess.

'Not just a look, is it? More a destroy.'

Theodora sniffed the air. It was stale with a slight tang of black tobacco but also some sweeter smell she'd met recently. Was it aftershave or scent? Then she remembered. 'Whoever did this may have done me and taken the cross.'

Tom looked at the mess. Then he went to the computer and turned it on. There was a flash from the screen and then nothing. He tried again. 'Either coincidence or they've sabotaged it. How do you destroy a memory?'

'I spend so much time trying not to on the parish

one at Geoffrey's, I really don't know. What's the way round?'

'We'd better try the other computers.'

'Teape's in the library,' Theodora offered.

'Let's try Clutch's first.'

In Myfannwy's bijou office all was to hand. Tom seated himself before the computer and switched on. Theodora was reminded of someone about to play an organ.

'There's a fortune to be made by the man who can invent a software package to persuade the clergy to use software packages,' Tom remarked. 'Perhaps I am that man,' he mused contentedly.

'Catch twenty-two,' Theodora snubbed him – she'd had enough of her ignorance being exposed for one night. 'They'd have to try before they'd be convinced, and if they're willing to try they're already convinced.'

'The thing is to find if there are files hidden away which could refer to the Azbarnah affair.' Tom was intent only on his task.

'Would Canon Clutch give any information to Mrs Gwynether?'

'Oh yes. He assumes everyone is utterly stupid and that they never make any inferences from the information he gives them. It's part of his feeling that he can make words mean what he wants them to mean – that he can form the world by describing it.'

'That's a theological way of defining God,' Theodora

smiled, and pushed him a box of disks to help him in his game.

'So my Methodist mentors always told me.'

Theodora felt herself rebuked. Why had she supposed that Tom had no religious background? After all, one would need some impulse to enter the service of the Church as a layman.

Tom fiddled from software to software through Microsoft to WordPerfect to Ami Pro. The everyday files were easy to penetrate. Mrs Gwynether had a penchant for whimsy: 'mite' housed expenses claims; 'talents', petty cash; 'Samaritan' located Overseas Mission; and a quick scroll through 'Jeremiah' revealed it was concerned with long-term financial forecasts. Tom slipped in disk after disk moving through old agenda and lots of letters to important people that Canon Clutch apparently could not bear to delete. Some were quite short, accepting or refusing invitations to the great and the good. Five recent ones within the last year bore an address at the Foreign Office to someone called Morely-Trump, Permanent Under Secretary.

Theodora stopped Tom. 'Hang on a moment, that's my FO relation. Can we check out what he's doing with Clutch?'

Slowly Tom scrolled through the letters. 'They seem to have spent a lot of time at somewhere called "Holdings" in Hampshire. Three weekends in a row this summer.'

'It's a large, cold Victorian house entirely

surrounded by watercress,' Theodora supplied. 'M-T inherited it from the other side of the family. I only went once. It's a pity we don't know what was discussed there. I can't honestly imagine M-T inviting someone like Clutch just for his charms.'

'Perhaps a case of religious conversion?' Tom was not serious.

'M-T is a Roman Catholic.' Theodora was austere.

'We really could do with a briefing paper or a memorandum to give us a narrative link,' Tom said, darting round the directories. 'Pity they don't use Apple Macs, they're so much more intuitive.'

Theodora loved his language. She gazed over his shoulder as the command came up: 'Password required.'

'Hah! Now, what would she use?'

'Azbarnah or bits of it?'

Tom typed all possible bits of Azbarnah. Nothing happened. Over the next ten minutes they tried 'Orthodoxy', 'Church', 'Truegrave', 'Archimandrite' and, in desperation, 'Irradium'.

Then Theodora said, 'How about "Genesis"?'

Up came the directory with files entitled 'Adam' and 'Eve'. They contained a log of Ecclesia Place responses to overtures from the Turannidi family over four years. They were political and financial in tone. Religion did not figure. They could have been negotiating land and commodities deals. The correspondence was meticulously dated and referenced.

Theodora let out a sigh. 'So that's it. Your supposition was absolutely right. The Foreign Office is simply using the Church of England to do its political will.'

Tom was jubilant. 'So, ho ho.' He cared less about the purity of the Church than she did, Theodora realised.

'How about "Exodus"?' she suggested.

The subfile was 'Moses and Aaron'. This was slightly better news as far as Theodora was concerned. It went into some detail about the ways in which the Church of England would support financially the restoration of church buildings and the training of priests in Vorasi seminary over the next seven years, together with an amount of one million pounds sterling to be given in four parts over the next four years for 'the furtherance of the Azbarnah Church's mission'. At the end was a list of guaranteed assets which looked to Tom remarkably like the list of objects that he'd seen that afternoon displayed at the Galaxy Gallery.

'Thirty pieces of silver,' said Theodora bitterly.

Tom leaned back in his chair and pushed his arms out behind him, triumph and tiredness combined.

'You know, there's nothing actually criminal in all this,' Theodora said.

'No. But one, we now have a reason why the concordat is so very important. And two, the Church of England as a whole might not exactly want its funds spent in this way just because the Government would like to get its hands on some cheap basic materials.'

'The idea is that the Church as a whole shouldn't know too much about it. All the concordat talks about as far as I can see is co-operation, unspecified, and intercommunion.'

'I thought we couldn't intercommunicate with Orthodoxy since we went for women priests.' Tom liked to get details straight.

'I get the feeling Azbarnah Orthodoxy goes its own way and if the Church of England's money is available, our doctrinal errors aren't going to stand in the way.'

'Greedy Church meets greedy Government,' Tom said.

'Nothing to choose between them.' Theodora was angry. 'Really, what a set of crooks they all are.'

'Yes,' Tom agreed, 'and we could still do with a body.'

'It needs to be properly mourned,' Theodora agreed. 'And I'd quite like to show the powers that be that the concordat wasn't properly signed and give the Diet an opportunity to debate the full facts so they can see just what they're putting their hand to and for whose benefit.'

'I'd like to know whether or not it was killed, murdered, or whether it had a heart attack.' Tom pursued his own interest. 'It's difficult to know what to do with this lot.' He gestured to the flickering light of the computer screen. 'If the FO wants the deal and Clutch does get the Diet to approve it and if Truegrave can get his way with the Orthodox

182

hierarchy and families out in Azbarnah and if we can't prove foul play, we're really rather stymied.'

'Archie Douglas,' said Theodora. 'The media shall be our salvation.'

CHAPTER THIRTEEN

The Boat

The rocking of the boat on the tide reminded Maggie of her dream of Eden. There were rivers in Eden, she seemed to recall.

'Couldn't live far from water, could you, boy?' She rested on her oars and addressed the empty seat in the stern. The nephew had grown older in the course of the week. He'd got more conversable. He was beginning to resemble that nice lad with the hogged mane who worked at the Place and gave her a civil time of day when they passed each other.

The current began to pluck at the craft. Just past midnight, Maggie reckoned the tide told her, and still flooding for another hour. The boat was wooden and heavy. It had been built of seasoned oak round about the turn of the century and well maintained year after year. She smelt the fresh smell of the latest coat of pitch on the gunwales. She didn't hold with these light plastic container things, so flimsy the current could spin them round.

'Always go with the tide. You've got to remember that,' she told him. 'There's a lot of power there and it's daft to fight it. Wait for the tide to turn and go with it.'

It was nice to have someone so attentive to pass your advice on to, she felt. As she pulled her craft straight with the starboard oar she could see the lights of Betterhouse Bridge and their dancing reflections on the water. The motor barge was a quarter of a mile upstream. No lights showed from the crumbling warehouses of the left bank; the right bank flashed with cars on the embankment. Far in her wake she could see the searchlight of the river police sweeping dutifully from side to side.

'It's a great highway, isn't it?' she said to her nephew. 'Like the M25, it takes you everywhere and back again.' The feeling went through her body of pull and push, drag and give. But the sensation was of water not land, river not people, and Maggie felt she could cope fine. She wouldn't have minded being a ferrywoman. 'Perhaps in another life, eh, boy?' Certainly she felt a lot steadier on her feet and in her wits when she'd done a stint on the river.

The boat began to feel the tug of the wash from the anchored barge. Maggie pulled efficiently round to the side nearest the bank, the Betterhouse side. She held the boat steady, raised an oar and banged on the metal side. It made a noise like thunder.

There was no waiting at all. A head peered over the rail and a rope dropped into her lap. She shipped her oars and made the rope fast to her own painter. Then she sat quietly feeling the rise and fall of the water and listening to the wood of her rowing boat creak and tap against the metal of the larger craft. After a minute or two she heard the sound of boots on iron and voices, one foreign, one upper-class English. A moment later a rope ladder snaked over the side and a dark form descended.

The English voice said, 'Hang on to Bernhardt.'

'Tash, I thank for your helping.'

'A pleasure. Keep your boots dry, old man.'

At ten to nine after early morning Mass, the last person Theodora wanted to encounter was Anona Trice. She was standing in the churchyard beside the table tomb with a trug in one hand and a hoe in the other. In the middle of Surrey perhaps, Theodora thought; in St Sylvester's Betterhouse graveyard, never.

'We have plans,' Anona turned her eager face towards her, 'to do up the churchyard, to make it a sanctuary, a green place for people to refresh themselves.' She indicated the dozen yards of matted grass at the roots of which glinted here and there the brown glass bottles of the wino platoon who irregularly met there of an evening. 'Don't you think it's a good idea?

Geoffrey thinks so. And Gilbert says it will be good for me.'

'Splendid,' said Theodora briskly. 'Just what we need to complete the church's renewal.' The roof and inside of St Sylvester had been restored the previous year. It had helped to increase the congregation.

'I thought chrysanthemums.' Anona pointed to a tray of weary looking cuttings at her side.

'Just the job.' Theodora endeavoured to keep walking. Her lack of charity towards Anona was a reproach to her but she felt it was a matter of self-preservation. It was as though Anona had a disease of which she could only be healed if she passed it on to someone else. And Theodora was damned if it was going to be her.

'And then we shall need to get the trees lopped.'

Theodora glanced up at the two good sized chestnuts marking the boundary of the churchyard. The boughs of one swept the earth, brushing the top of the table tomb and its lachrymose angels. She stopped. Hanging from the bough, swinging to and fro in the light breeze, was a glint of silver and blue. Hesitantly she approached it.

'Hell's teeth,' she said angrily to Anona over her shoulder. 'Where did you find that?'

'It came my way,' Anona's tone was complacent, 'and it seemed a good place for it to rest, with him to whom it belongs.'

Theodora stared at her with incomprehension. Anona tapped the tomb. 'He's at peace,' she said. 'All

quite proper. Bernhardt will come back now. I shall be
here to greet him when he comes.'

The *Express* had banner headlines (it being a poor
season for news): 'Clergy Corpse in Churchyard –
Church Chiefs Cheat on Contract?' Theodora felt she
wasn't up to the *Express*'s treatment and turned to
the more muted tones of the *Telegraph*. The story
had made the front page but lower down, below the
headlines on the latest Serbian atrocities. Under the
heading 'Mystery of the Missing Archimandrite' it
read: 'The four-day-old corpse of a middle-aged man
wearing clerical dress was found yesterday morning
in a tomb in the churchyard of St Sylvester's Betterhouse, South-East London. The body has been ident-
ified as that of the Archimandrite of Azbarnah,
Georgios XII. Millions of TV viewers saw someone
they took to be the Archimandrite with the Archbishop of York, Michael Papworth, interviewed on
News at Ten by Archie Douglas on Monday night.
Now doubt is being cast on the veracity of that appearance. Information from a source close to Ecclesia
Place suggests that the Archimandrite was dead
some hours before that interview. According to the
airline authorities, the Archimandrite, who was due
to fly out on Tuesday morning, did not do so but the
staff of the Galaxy Gallery (Very thorough, thought
Theodora, not a stone unturned) reported that someone they took to be the Archimandrite was at the
Azbarnah exhibition for a short time on Wednesday

afternoon. The Azbarnah authorities, who have an office in the Moldavian Consulate, were unavailable for comment last night. Investigations are continuing.'

In other words, if nothing better turns up, the thing will run and run. Theodora ran her eye down the column. 'The Archimandrite came to Ecclesia Place, Westminster, HQ of the Church of England, on Monday afternoon. He is supposed to have signed a contract for closer relations between the Azbarnah Orthodox Church and the C of E. But if the Ecclesia Place source is correct and the Archimandrite was dead before the signing took place and a substitute signed for him, then that contract might not be legally valid. The chief secretary to the Diet, Canon Ken Clutch (Theodora thought she liked the chumminess of the shortened first name for Clutch), was being questioned last night by Inspector Semper of the Metropolitan Police. The Diet's Eastern European affairs expert, Rev. Bernhardt Truegrave, is wanted for questioning.' Where was Teape in all this? Theodora wondered. Cowering down in his crypt archive?

'A spokeswoman for Lambeth Palace said the Archbishop of Canterbury considered it was very important for all Christians to co-operate with governments to work together for a better world and both the Church of England and the Azbarnah Orthodox Church had a part to play. (So he knew, Theodora thought.) The Archbishop of York is on holiday. A spokesman for the Foreign Office, Mr Julian Morely-Trump, said that HM Government had no knowledge of the relations of the Church of England with Azbarnah and the matter was entirely one for the Church authorities.'

The Times had a seemly account of the discovery of the body by Anona and Theodora and a background article on Azbarnah, complete with map for the ignorant, focusing on Azbarnah's aspirations within the new Europe.

The *Independent* had added a third leader on the wisdom of naive church authorities playing politics and guessing they'd been made the tool of the FO.

Really, Theodora thought with pride, Archie had surpassed her expectations, all things considered. If the Church wanted to cut a figure in the political arena and told itself the media were very important, it would have to take the rough with the smooth.

It had been a heavy twenty-four hours since she and Geoffrey had lifted the stone slab from the tomb and gazed into the waxy face of the Archimandrite. She had escorted Anona back to the Foundation and entrusted her to Gilbert's care while Geoffrey got the police. Together they had given the police all possible assistance but, that done, parish priorities had reasserted themselves. Geoffrey had refused to cancel the funeral of a defunct Rotarian due to be buried just before lunch and had got the police to clear the churchyard of reporters, TV men and sightseers. Professionally, she felt Geoffrey had done rather well. Though the Rotarian's family had been surprised at the large turnout. They seemed to have coped at parish level rather better than the top brass, who had to hide behind a screen of spokesmen denying and denying.

Theodora had done as she had promised Tom. She'd rung Morely-Trump, after Mass and before breakfast, while the papers were still only headlines on the table. She wondered if Julian had seen the papers and the Azbarnah drama or not. If he was out of the country, he might have missed them. Communication had not been easy. She had begun with the Foreign Office. Manners were impeccable but actual contact regrettably impossible. 'Mr Morely-Trump is on leave at present. Who is calling?'

'His cousin.' Theodora settled for the description. The slight pause at the other end hinted at disbelief. 'When does he return?' she inquired.

There was a sound of flicking pages. 'The twenty-third of this month.'

'Has he left a contact number?'

'I'm terribly sorry but it isn't our practice to give out private numbers.'

'Thank you.' Theodora echoed the austerity of the secretary's tone.

Where do Foreign Office members take their holidays? She consulted her own address book under 'Family' and dialled the Hampshire number.

It was answered at once. 'Julian Morely-Trump

speaking.' In the background was the sharp, high sound of small dogs barking.

'Julian, Theodora here. Theodora Braithwaite.'

Julian was not a diplomat for nothing. There was no pause. 'Theo, how very nice to hear you. It's years, isn't it, six or seven at least. Uncle Hugh's eightieth, wasn't it?'

'Yes.'

'Do you keep up? Is he well?' Julian clearly thought she'd rung to announce Canon Hugh Braithwaite's death.

'So far as I know he's well. I had a card last week. Julian, it's not family I'm ringing about. More business.' Would he suppose she wanted to borrow money? The Morely-Trump side of the family were known to the Braithwaites to be thrifty, even, it was murmured, mean. The barking reached a crescendo. 'Shut up, you two.' Julian's Wykehamist tones couldn't rise to shouting down his dogs. What would they be? Pekes? West Highlands? They had that edge of hysteria which small dogs seemed to run to.

'Can you hang on a minute, Theo? I'll switch to the study. It'll be a bit quieter.'

There was series of clicks, the sound of a dog's yap cut off suddenly and then silence. Theodora tried to recall the details of the Hampshire house. At fourteen she'd been taken there in term time from Cheltenham for a family gathering. She remembered windows obscured by Virginia creeper creating a green light in the long rooms and a consequent feeling of being underwater. This impression was enhanced by the number of tall, dark plants, potted palms and aspidistras, which stood in corners and cascaded out of huge Oriental vases. Had Julian cleared them out when he inherited the house or was he swimming towards his study through their subaqueous light?

'Hello? That's better. Now, business, you were saying.'

The background noise was certainly reduced though she could still hear the powerful tick of a pendulum clock. It brought the study back to her. She remembered it as book-lined and Turkey-carpeted with a smell of liniment because Julian's mother had ridden to hounds well into her eighties and kept herself supple by the lavish application of the stuff both on her mounts and herself. Theodora found herself inhaling the mouth piece to see if the smell was still there.

'Azbarnah.' Theodora saw no reason for beating about bushes.

'A rebarbative country,' Julian offered.

'And people.'

Julian was noncommital.

'And Church.'

'So I could imagine. The bits of Orthodoxy I've met in my travels always seemed fairly ferocious.'

'I knew some rather gentle and spiritual ones at Oxford,' Theodora volunteered. 'Perhaps they weren't typical.'

'The ones I know have long hair and cutlasses between their teeth.'

'They don't seem to know the difference between religion and politics.' Theodora wondered if Julian himself was familiar with that difference. Would his Roman Catholic allegiance provide him with that distinction?

'The Church lives in the world.' Julian was a convert, one of Monsignor Gilbey's young Cambridge team.

'Have you been there?' she asked.

'As it happens I haven't but I gather I'm being sent, all being well, some time in the New Year.'

'And the Orthodox Church there is a big property owner, isn't it?'

'Theo, what is all this?'

Theodora turned the *Independent* over on the table in front of her. 'Have you seen the papers this morning?'

'Actually no. I'm using my leave to finish my book. My editor is making a nuisance of himself.'

Theodora was interested. 'What are you doing?'

'It's a life of Busonvici the Bearded. Don't pretend you've ever heard of him.'

'The sources will be in old high Slavonic.' Theodora was pleased with herself. Tom's potted history of Azbarnah was fresh in her mind. 'He evangelised Azbarnah in the thirteenth century.'

Julian was clearly miffed to find himself the victim of this one-upmanship. 'How come you're such an expert on the early history of Azbarnah? Or,' inspiration smote him, 'have you been to the little exhibition at the Galaxy?'

'No, but I keep up. The clerical network.' He must surely know about that. The family as a whole had a formidable one. 'I gather you know Canon Clutch.'

There was a silence. At last she'd got home. She could hear the tick of the clock in the study.

'A mere acquaintance.'

'Four times at Holdings this summer.'

'How on earth?'

'Julian, today's *Independent* reads . . .' Theodora filled him in on the events connected with the death of the Archimandrite and the consequent row at Ecclesia Place. She could tell by his voice he was shaken. If she hadn't been family she suspected he would have put the phone down murmuring 'no comment'. As it was, he took his time.

Finally he said, 'Theo, strictly between ourselves, there are national interests at stake here. HM Government has a policy initiative in place, which means we don't want any trouble with the Azbarnah authorities at this moment in time.'

'Does this mean you've suborned the gullible and snobbish Clutch to do your dirty work for you?'

'Those aren't quite the terms we'd use. I would remind you that the Church of England is a national church. It has to pay for its special, established status by co-operating with Government policy in some areas.'

'Time we disestablished.'

'Not a view your Archbishops share with you.'

'They may modify their opinion if this shambles runs on.'

Family supervened over diplomat. 'Yes, I fear you may be right. I suppose there is nothing you can do to help us. You seem terribly well-informed. I remember you always were. You should have gone into the Service.'

'In a sense I did. Just a different service. And no, actually, I haven't the power to do anything to help the Government even if I wanted to. But just for the record, are all the Ecclesia Place top brass in on this?'

She could hear him bite back his professional no comment. 'We got hold of Clutch early on and he suggested we use Truegrave's band of hunters. And in fact they really were extremely useful. I doubt if we could have done without them. The Archimandrite's family runs the whole show, as you may have gathered. They own the land and fill the main offices of state, such as they are.'

'What about Teape?'

'Yes, he was a pain. He found out what was going on and the price of compliance was that he should have first offer on various little *objets d'art* from the Azbarnahi Church treasury. He's a greedy little fellow, isn't he?'

'With hollow heels?'

'It has been known.'

'And do I gather you bring in your Azbarnahi

contacts by boat every now and again? Dutch motor barge with a German flag up the Thames to Betterhouse?'

'Really, Theo, you exceed,' Julian had said as he put the phone down. 'Give my love to Uncle Hugh when you write next.'

Theodora laid the newspapers on her new table. It was, she had to admit, useful and comfortable. The room, her room, her space, looked splendid, bare, clean, sanded, books in place, autumn sun slanting through the open windows; a good high tide for the springs. Now that the affair was almost over she had ventured upon a modest house warming. Archie had said he would be delighted. Tom would come with pleasure. Oenone had answered for Geoffrey and hoped they would be able to look in. Wrestling with conscience, she had invited Anona. Gilbert had answered the phone and replied rather austerely that Anona was indisposed. She'd had a long session with Inspector Semper of the Metropolitan Police. No, he very much regretted he himself was not available, though of course he wished Theodora every blessing in her new abode. Would she want prayers said, holy water sprinkled? Theodora was touched. Any time at his convenience. They parted, apparently friends.

Theodora wondered if she had enough food for Tom and looked at her watch to see if she had time to dash out for more cheese. There were industrial amounts of cold pasta, green salad, olive bread, *pecorino*, Stilton, Coxes, blackberry and apple pie kindly contributed by a parishioner she'd visited regularly in hospital and who, on her release, had embarked on an orgy of cooking by way of celebration. It was Tom she was worried about, a growing lad.

The sound of voices in the Stowage below resolved the question.

'Theo, dearie,' Archie said, holding her in one arm and a bottle in the other. They seemed to have become more familiar than Theodora remembered to be the case. Though possibly it was simply the style of the media. He put the champagne on the table and looked round. 'Nice little place you've got yourself. Should be worth a mint in five years, these river houses. Love the smell of Rentokil.'

'Archie,' Theodora genuinely felt gratitude, 'it is good to see you, I mean in the flesh after all this time. And champagne! You shouldn't have.'

'I owe you, sweetie. The Ecclesia Place mess is an absolute dream. Won me lots and lots of useful friends and interesting enemies. Do you know a man called Morely-Trump? Amazing how eager people are to put the boot into the poor old C of E.'

Theodora dolefully agreed.

'Well, the top brass really are so pig stupid. They should stick to religion.'

Tom bounded into the room. He held a good-looking ham wrapped in cellophane, clearly not trusting Theodora's ordnance. 'Feared you might be vegetarian,' he said honestly. 'Will my bike be all right chained to your rails?'

'With the number of police spread over Betterhouse at the moment, I think it might be.'

'Goody.' Tom looked at the table spread with approval. 'Who else is coming?'

'You know Archie Douglas.'

'I do now.' They smiled at each other. Perhaps they might like each other. Theodora preferred her friends to get on.

'I'm really grateful for all that insider info on Ecclesia Place. It sounds absolutely incredible.'

'As an organisation it could really do with a SWOT analysis,' Tom was embarked and earnest, 'but of course you can only do that, one, against a set of agreed aims and two, with the full co-operation of the personnel. Neither of which . . .'

'Ah,' said Archie, always eager for new knowledge but a bit out of his depth. Theodora for once positively welcomed Oenone's light tapping on the stairs.

'Theo, and Archie Douglas, isn't it? And Mr Logg, Tom, I assume. How very nice to meet you in the flesh at last. We've heard so much about you.' Oenone took charge. 'I know you've no ice, Theo, so we've brought some for the wine.' She indicated Geoffrey staggering through the door with what appeared to be a hamper. Theodora hadn't seen one of those in years. Glasses were filled.

'To our hostess in her new house,' said Geoffrey. Theodora allowed herself to think how very charming Geoffrey was and suppressed the thought that he was wasted on Oenone.

'Now,' said Oenone, drawing them round her in Theodora's room. 'Geoffrey and I want to know all about it. Who, for example, has been interviewed by the police?'

'I have,' Archie, Tom and Theodora answered together.

'Tell,' said Oenone to Archie.

'Well,' said Archie, 'a man called Inspector Semper tracked me down at the *Independent* about lunchtime yesterday, Thursday. I'd just sold the idea of an article on the C of E being used by politicians for political ends as per instruction,' he nodded at Theodora, 'when this chap Semper turned up fresh from unearthing your Archimandrite from his tomb in your churchyard.' He grinned at Geoffrey. 'Well, of course I had to reveal my sources.'

'Which led the excellent inspector to me,' Tom took up. 'Sources close to Ecclesia Place, as they say. I must admit I had a really most agreeable time with Semper. He seemed to me to be remarkably quick on the uptake, not at all like the police I met as a student.'

Theodora wondered what police those would have been. Perhaps he had peddled his bicycle furiously in Reading in a built-up area. *pedalled*

'Well,' Tom was pressing on, 'I was all for doing it very quietly and offered to take him to the Calf and have a private chat. He didn't want that. He made quite an interesting remark, I thought, about the need for openness and how it "might do the top brass good to see that nothing could now be hidden." In fact he quoted Latin at me which I didn't quite get. *"Nil inulta remanebit"?'* Tom looked at Theodora.

'It's a line from the Dies Irae, a canticle sometimes sung at a Requiem Mass. It speaks of the Day of Judgement on which nothing shall remain unavenged. What a very educated policeman, or perhaps a Roman Catholic. And how apposite!'

'So we did it in style.' Tom took pleasure in the memory. 'He got Ashwood to show him up and told him to ring Clutch and tell him that when he'd finished with me he'd like to have a word with him. By the time he'd come up the main staircase and penetrated to my loft, his presence was all over the Place. Of course there was nothing at that point generally known about the discovery of the body.'

'So what were you able to tell him?' Oenone kept him on task.

'I told him about my finding the body and then losing it. I told him about the photograph of the true Archimandrite and the presence of the false one. I told him about the machinations of the C of E which their records suggest have been prompted by the Foreign Office for strictly nonreligious ends.'

'And what was his response?' Geoffrey was curious.

'He clearly thinks he can get us all, at the very least, on the grounds of failing to report a death, i.e. tell them about the body. He wants more proof as to the canon or canons having moved it after I had moved it. Also there is something about impersonating, but he wasn't too clear whether that was an offence. I think he feels impersonating foreigners doesn't count. And anyway I didn't know anything about the impersonation until much later and if Clutch knew about it, he would only be assisting in it. They'd have to find the false Archimandrite and take him in.'

'Dear me, does that mean they'll prosecute you?'

'Oh, I do hope so.' Tom was enthusiastic. 'The whole prison culture thing, a closed institution, is absolutely fascinating. Lots and lots of research to be done in that area. And of course it would be interesting to see how Clutch etc reacted to prison conditions.'

'I had a friend who did a stretch at Ford,' Archie said conversationally. 'He said it was far more exclusive than your average public school nowadays.'

'And more comfortable,' Geoffrey offered.

'Not hard,' agreed Archie, who thought of his hideous years at Loretto.

'Can't they do anything else to put an end to Clutch and Co.?' Was she being vindictive? Theodora wondered.

'It isn't an offence apparently to work for the Foreign Office's interests.' Archie was dry.

'Not even if you don't declare to your own institution that that is what you're doing?' Oenone was indignant. In some ways, Theodora thought, Oenone had an absolutely straightforward sense of honour which had nothing to do with social advancement.

'That's for the Church to decide, as Morely-Trump might say.'

'Much depends on how the Archimandrite died.' Tom held out some hope for the women. 'At the moment they don't know. If it wasn't natural causes, we may all of us be in a different establishment from Ford.'

'How did the body get from the Place to the tomb?' Archie inquired.

Theodora looked at Geoffrey. 'Will you or shall I?'

'I do feel responsible for Anona,' Geoffrey said.

'We *all* feel responsible for Anona,' Theodora reassured him. 'It's a way she has. She's terribly successful at it.'

'Anona was married to Truegrave.' Geoffrey got to the point. 'The marriage broke up three years ago.'

Oenone leaned forward and said in a low voice to Theodora as though it might be offensive to the gentlemen, 'She found he preferred men to women.'

'I'm amazed he could be acceptable to either,' Theodora murmured back.

'She's never really got to terms with it,' Geoffrey went on. 'Gilbert says she talks about waiting and how important it is to keep actively waiting, sort of concentrating on the objects of affection to such a point of intensity that they are drawn back to you.'

'I've known Labradors like that,' Oenone contributed. 'They concentrate so hard on a dish on the table that that dish is drawn towards them.'

Theodora thought how love blinds even intelligent men since Geoffrey appeared to find this fatuousness perfectly acceptable. 'Well,' he continued, 'she devised a plan to draw Bernhardt back to her by getting hold of things he might want.'

'The cross,' Theodora offered.

'Gilbert knew about that.' Geoffrey was almost apologetic. 'She apparently came over here to your flat one lunchtime, it must have been Tuesday, and found the door had been forced. She asserted that the cross was lying around.'

'A gross distortion of the truth!' Theodora exclaimed. 'She must have gone through my Barbour pockets to find it. It is quite incredible that the local talent should break in and take nothing from me but that a churchwoman married to a senior cleric should stoop to thieving.'

Tom thought her values were most attractive and unusual. He smiled and hoped to hear more.

'How did she connect it with the body?' Archie wanted to know.

'Maggie found the body,' Tom said unexpectedly. 'Semper shared that fact with me. Or at least he didn't quite put it like that. He said that traces of boat pitch had been found on the suiting of the Archimandrite and these had been traced to a rowing boat which is used by Maggie.'

'So she came across it in the rubbish outside the Place on Monday night?' Theodora said.

'Of course, it would look quite reasonable to Maggie to put it in a tomb in a churchyard. After all, that's where bodies usually go.' Tom liked the rationality of the thing.

'Where Anona found it,' Theodora concluded.

'No. Maggie was friendly with Anona,' Geoffrey said. 'They used to go on boat trips together in Maggie's dinghy. Maggie thinks the river has healing qualities. She saw Anona's need and catered for it. So when she'd brought the Archimandrite's body on its last journey, she pottered across to the Foundation and rooted out Anona to give her a hand at the burial in the tomb.'

'But Anona said something about Bernhardt coming and finding it there. What did she mean?'

'Anona knew quite a lot about Bernhardt's affairs and his movements. I gather she was in and out of the Place fairly often. She knew that he was heavily involved with Azbarnahi affairs.'

'The smell,' said Theodora suddenly. 'The smell in my room and the smell in Truegrave's office. It was Anona's scent. She did his office over.'

'Right. And what she found was that a deal had been struck with one of the Turannidi scions.'

'To the effect that?' Archie leaned forward.

The telephone bell startled them. Theodora leaned over. 'It's for you,' she said to Tom. 'Inspector Semper.'

No one made any attempt not to listen.

When he had finished, Tom turned back to them.

'They've found he died from a heart attack.'
    'So you probably won't go to prison,' Oenone said.
    'Pity,' said Tom. 'Some other time I hope.'

Obsequies

'Political power is not the same as spiritual power.'

The cold draught ruffled the leaves of the sober wreaths and the white lilies which decorated the church. The west window of St Sylvester's caught the pale November light and refracted it through the greens and golds of the Kempe design to make a carpet of blurred colour on the floor under the tower.

'Only death comes from confusing them.' Geoffrey's quiet tone had no trace of rhetoric. He spoke the sober truth, Theodora thought as she watched him from her deacon's stall. It had been a difficult service to arrange, she'd heard. The Diocesan had been told to have a memorial service for someone he had never met, the Archimandrite of Azbarnah, and of whom, she suspected, he might not have approved. He'd rung the Foreign Office for help and got someone called Morely-Trump who had emphasised that relations with Azbarnah were really terribly important and that since the Church had made such a mess of them, it would indeed be only civil to hold some sort of service in memory of the dead prelate. Though of course it was entirely a matter for the Church. The Diocesan had done his best. He'd had a long discussion with Geoffrey; he'd been briefed by the Archbishop. He'd thought of ringing Ecclesia Place for help but then remembered. Canon Clutch had had a heart attack and was in hospital. Canon Truegrave's tragic accident in the private plane of a member of the Turannidi family over Mount Dovraki had taken him from the scene. As for Canon Teape, there had been silence at the end of the telephone. It had emerged that the Canon was in a remand prison, something to do with evasion of customs duty on antique stolen goods.

'Political power,' Geoffrey continued, 'is imposed from without, spiritual power comes from within. Political power rests ultimately on force and fear; fear that we shall lose something precious to us. But mortal spoils cannot save us. What can be taken from us was never ours, never precious or worthy in the first place. *Religious* power, on the other hand, working within our very souls, stems from God alone, Who is closer to us than our own skin.'

Theodora looked down at the scattering of disparate souls sitting well apart from each other in the huge church. At the back were five slab-faced men in fur coats who she supposed must be representing the Azbarnah side of things. Nearer the front she glimpsed Anona, wearing a black headscarf framing a pallid face and vacant eyes, sitting next to Gilbert Racy who

looked lost in prayer. On Anona's other side sat
Oenone gazing supportively at her husband. Behind
her in a new-looking overcoat was Tom Logg, taking it
all in, interested, curious about someone else's work
space. She felt a rush of gratitude that there were such
innocent, uncorrupted souls as Tom still about. Next to
him, looking pious, was Archie Douglas. It was really
rather good of him to turn out given that he was now
such a rising figure on the box.

'The *political* life, the life of the secular world, is the
life which builds up the ego from the outside, which
tempts us to define ourselves by our talents or
possessions or place, by the amount of fear we can
inspire in others, by the number of people we can
coerce. The *religious* life is the steady effort to erode
that grasping ego, from the inside, through the life of
prayer and discipline. It is the Church's task to teach
us how to live that religious life. It is the Church's *only*
task; it is only the *Church's* task.'

Theodora thought of Canon Clutch who had followed
his ego to the point where he had become the creature
of his own vanity and made himself the willing tool of
people who had far from religious ends. She thought of
Canon Truegrave who had wanted to be a power in
some strange political land. She thought of Canon
Teape who had collected church silver and wanted to
enlarge his collection so much that he'd not cared at all
about the means of doing so. They had seen death, the
death of a priest, as an inconvenience, an irritating
accident to be got round. They'd shuffled the body of a

human being around as though it were meat. And in so
doing they degraded both it and themselves. Tomorrow
the Diet would vote to decide whether and in what
form the connection with the Azbarnah Orthodox
Church would continue. Would politics or religion pre-
vail? she wondered.

Theodora was aware of two late entrants. Maggie
was shuffling down the south aisle followed by – who
would that be? Of course, Trace, Kevin, from the servants of Ecclesia Place, the poor who shall inherit the
earth. How very nice to see them. She wondered if she
should offer Maggie her basement for the winter as an
alternative to the bench outside the Place.

She meditated on the nature of political power
within the Church which she loved. Of course it was a
temptation to bishops and senior clergy besought by
the importunate media to *say*, and by desperate politicians to *do* something which would heal the world's
ills. But what was the point of Christianity if it could
not help them to resist such temptations, to reject the
urgencies of the world? All the Church could properly
say was, pray, reflect on scripture, cleanse and renew
yourself through the sacraments and only then should
you act. What TV commentator, what politician would
want to hear, would comprehend, such advice? The
world wanted instant remedies on its own terms.
Bishops should not pander to such desires but did.
They took their purple and their privileges and paid
the world in Caesar's coin. No wonder they came a
cropper.

She glanced up at the memorial plaque for Thomas Henry Newcome who lay buried in the chancel of this Church of St Sylvester which he had spent his fortune to build. The inscription read: 'In memory of Thomas Henry Newcome 1820–1891 who by his life and doctrine set forth God's true and lively word.' It was a simple epitaph for a complex character. He had founded a religious order the purpose of which was to support parish priests in poor areas. What would he have made of this strutting of clergy on national and international stages where they were only too likely to be duped by men far more unscrupulous than they? She thought of Geoffrey about whose talents and priorities she had no doubt. But where would Oenone steer him? And where, she was beginning to wonder, did her own path lie? How and where could she most fruitfully contribute?

'The key is freedom,' Geoffrey was concluding. 'In the end, political power must fail, for we must embrace freely, and without the coercion of fear or desire, the life of worship, the life lived towards God. Unless we can freely choose to do this, all is dust and ashes.'

Theodora thought of her almost empty house. Was that a step in the right direction?

More Crime Fiction from Headline

AN ECCLESIASTICAL WHODUNNIT

CLERICAL ERRORS

D. M. Greenwood

In the shadow of honey-coloured Medewich Cathedral, amidst the perfect lawns of the Cathedral Close, the diocesan office of St Manicus should have been a peaceful if not an especially exciting place for nineteen-year-old Julia Smith to start her first job. Yet she has been in its precincts for less than an hour when she stumbles on a horror of Biblical proportions – a severed head in the Cathedral font.

And she has worked for the suave Canon Wheeler for less than a day when she realises that the Dean and Chapter is as riven by rivalry, ambition and petty jealousy as the court of any Renaissance prelate. In this jungle of intrigue a young deaconess, Theodora Braithwaite, stands out as a lone pillar of common sense. Taciturn but kindly, she takes Julia under her wing, and with the assistance of Ian Caretaker – a young man who hates Canon Wheeler as much as he loves the Church – they attempt to unravel the truth behind the death of a well-meaning man, the Reverend Paul Gray, late incumbent of Markham cum Cumbermound.

FICTION / CRIME 0 7472 3582 1

More Crime Fiction from Headline

CAROLINE GRAHAM

'An exemplary crime novel' *The Literary Review*

DEATH OF A HOLLOW MAN

For Detective Chief Inspector Tom Barnaby a visit to the Causton Amateur Dramatic Society's production of *Amadeus* is not an ideal evening's entertainment. But loyalty to his wife Joyce (noises-off), means that attending the first night is a must, and Barnaby knows that an immense amount of hard work has gone into the show.

Backstage, nerves are fraying. Director of the play, Harold Winstanley, has introduced a strict pecking order among the cast but the leading man is taking his role far too much to heart. Esslyn Carmichael), suspecting that his wife is having an affair, has decided that the stage is as good a place as any to wring the truth out of the guilty party. It is his final act, though, that proves to be a *pièce de résistance* and when the scene takes a particularly gruesome turn, Barnaby finds that his professional skills are called to the fore.

Superbly plotted and sparkling with vivid characters, *Death of a Hollow Man* is a first-class whodunnit that brings the author to the very front of her field.

'Excellent character sketches of the suspects, and the dialogue is lively and convincing' *Independent*

'Tension builds, bitchery flares, resentment seethes ... Lots of atmosphere, colourful characters and fair clues' *Mail on Sunday*

FICTION / CRIME 0 7472 3350 0

A selection of bestsellers from Headline

All Headline books are available at your local bookshop or newsagent, or can be ordered direct from the publisher. Just tick the titles you want and fill in the form below. Prices and availability subject to change without notice.

Headline Book Publishing, Cash Sales Department, Bookpoint, 39 Milton Park, Abingdon, OXON, OX14 4TD, UK. If you have a credit card you may order by telephone – 01235 400400.

Please enclose a cheque or postal order made payable to Bookpoint Ltd to the value of the cover price and allow the following for postage and packing:

UK & BFPO: £1.00 for the first book, 50p for the second book and 30p for each additional book ordered up to a maximum charge of £3.00.

OVERSEAS & EIRE: £2.00 for the first book, £1.00 for the second book and 50p for each additional book.

Name ....

Address ....

....

....

If you would prefer to pay by credit card, please complete:
Please debit my Visa/Access/Diner's Card/American Express (delete as applicable) card no:

Signature .... Expiry Date ....